The Art of Farming

The Art of Farming

SKETCHES OF A LIFE IN THE COUNTRY

A NOVEL

WRITTEN AND ILLUSTRATED BY
T.D MOTLEY

Stoney Creek Publishing

Published by

Stoney Creek Publishing Group

StoneyCreekPublishing.com

ISBN: 979-8-9901289-3-4
ISBN (paperback): 979-8-9901289-1-0
ISBN (ebook): 979-8-9901289-2-7
Library of Congress Control Number: 2024912444

Cover design by Market Your Industry, MarketYourIndustry.com. Cover illustration: *Cornfield at Sunset* by T.D. Motley

Printed in the United States

For Becca, Sharon and Wyndi

This book would not have happened without you.

About 24,000 years ago, humans started painting pictures of animals and farming the landscape.
Just in time for this story about a modern artist who became a farmer.

Contents

Introduction

"Samuel Bartlett!" one of three beleaguered clerks called loudly.

"Here." I replied, while rising from a rickety folding chair, my hand raised like a schoolboy. I followed like one, too, and may have even timidly folded my hands behind my back. I wanted to make a good impression.

The lobby of the county tax assessor's office was packed with farmers, ranchers, feed store owners, implement and hardware dealers, and small-town business purveyors. Folding chairs had been brought in to accommodate the throng of tax-paying citizenry. It was that time of year.

Though a bit worn at the edges, the impressive late-nineteenth-century red stone courthouse made Elysia seem more continental, more *European,* than other towns in Barnes County. Suggesting a medieval fortress or castle, the historic looking structure was designed by a student of famed architect, J. Riely Gordon. Not as grand as Gordon's magnificent edifice in Waxahachie, the little Romanesque Revival style gem commanded admiration from visitors to that bucolic tip of the North Texas plains. It held its own against the Goliathan proportions of the newer Colonial style First Baptist Church down the street.

The tall round-arched windows resembled rows of Roman sentries, as if guarding the proud structure. Cone-capped slender turrets climbed as high as the central nave's deeply pitched gable, suggesting stone-clad grain silos reaching to the heavens. As an artist, I am particularly taken with the numerous carved foliate-heads, depictions of the ancient Green Man, that keep watch over the various portals of the courthouse.

I had recently retired from teaching art at a not-too-distant county community college. In the last few years of that career, I bought a small farmstead in the country. I was dipping my toes into the historic waters of rural farm life that had been practiced by my Texas family and ancestors since the early nineteenth century.

As I crossed the old lobby floor, ancient joists creaked and groaned below my footfall. Above, rusty pressed-tin florid ceiling tiles, circa 1930, had been expedient and cheap fire damage replacement for the lost original plaster decor. I nodded morning greetings to the local game processor and taxidermist, and one of my neighbors who baled gorgeous alfalfa hay for horses. Both were waiting their turns for taxation judgement. This was a yearly communal ritual, with biblical overtones.

I was familiar with the agent who greeted me, as he annually renewed my ag exemption, granted to me mainly for the few head of livestock I raised and sold at market each year. He ushered me into his updated office, furnished in an attempted mid-century modern style. Avocado-colored chair cushions were prominent. "Sam," he said simply. "Have a seat."

His greeting seemed a little more formal, at least less chatty, than usual. I suspected the reason, and I detected a slight frown on his forehead, as he perused the most recent review pages in my farm file. "OK..." he said, pausing to purse his lips a bit before continuing.

"We recognize that as you've expanded your chicken flock considerably, your eggs are selling well at the Farmer's Market." Another pause. He looked up at me for eye contact. "The wife bought some of your motley-colored eggs on Saturday." With a forced grin, he added "Kinda pricey, Sam. But I guess you are paying a lot for all this ORganic feed and scratch you're using."

"Damn right." I thought, but answered "Yes, Bob. The heritage breed hens lay colored eggs, very popular. And they are organic, as are all my herbs and produce, most of which are from heirloom seeds."

Bob retorted, with some authority, "Well my Daddy always taught us that you just can't beat the laying production of White Leghorns....but I acknowledge that customers today want choices. So, there's that." The last few words trailed off into a kind of lyrical, all-knowing hum, which was just Bob's way.

We'd arrived at the moment of truth, my purpose, to further demonstrate to the powers that be, that I was not simply running a "hobby farm." The livestock and chickens were one thing, but I was seeking further ag exemption consideration for my organic *heirloom* herbs and produce acreage. I put on my teacher's hat and launched ahead with my lecture, albeit to a class of only one skeptical county bureaucrat. My purpose was to justify my exploration into the then brave new world of organic farming, with heirloom produce and heritage breed livestock, to boot.

I was a bit of an odd duck in Elysia. But then I'd been one of those since childhood. I was a kid who aspired to being an artist, raised in a family of Texas farmers. My cousins went on to earn degrees in agriculture from places like Texas A&M. I earned graduate degrees in studio art and art history. For a couple of decades, I taught those very subjects at a Barnes County Community College, thirty minutes' drive from Elysia and environs.

I will say that I seem to have found new-born respect from my relatives, now that I've come back to farming, as it were. My cousins are not so sure about this organic herb and produce business I'm getting myself into. But they are relieved that I've finally left city life and returned to the country, the landscape of my childhood.

Sol, the miniature donkey

ONE

Portraits, Paddocks and Poultry

Clara and her pal were at the farm on Saturday. I'm boarding her tall and handsome Buckskin, Pickle, and Tofu, a little filly the color of dark chocolate, the same color as my big Bay, Samson. Tofu belongs to Margaret, Clara's vegetarian friend. Both are sophomores, and upon turning sixteen, each of their Texas farm/hardship drivers' licenses for fourteen- and fifteen-year-olds recently converted to the real thing, a genuine Texas driver's license, so their parents let them drive each other back and forth to the farm, all on local county or farm-to-market roads, of course.

Clara drives her Dad's old, dented Ford 250 truck. It still has a decent trailer-hitch capacity, so she's always pleading that I teach her good driving tricks for hauling horse-trailers, and maneuvering same, forwards and backwards and parking. I tell her the hard part is really learning how to coax any critter, be it equine, bovine, porcine, or ovine, to get into or out of a trailer when you want them to. They'll eventually do it, but never on your schedule.

My Samson is 16.3 hands high. He's mostly quarter horse, with some racehorse in him. His performance days are long past, but he still enjoys taking the youngsters for a ride, letting them practice. I built a small arena and a big round pen for the kids, my own, and the neighbors'.

The three-year-old filly is a beautiful horse, and very smart. Margaret has always been patient with her, even on routines requiring seemingly endless repetitions. The teen cowgirl loves Samson and is not shy about proudly pointing out that little Tofu and he look like clones, color-wise.

My longtime girlfriend, Annie, stayed the weekend. We call ourselves "sidekicks." A great cook, who loves harvesting straight from the garden to the kitchen, Annie made lunch for everybody. She baked her famous North Carolina Tomato Pie, following her favorite aunt's recipe, hand-written in a florid cursive that was common long ago. The savory pie was served with a big, tossed salad of rocket arugula, sweet basil, spinach and pecans, all ingredients from our gardens, of course. Annie appreciated Margaret's independent no-meat commitment, despite being raised in a ranching family. Annie is great with girls, and my own daughter, Liz, adores her.

We ate in the abundant shade of a giant 150-year-old white oak tree in the back yard of the 1912 Greek Revival style bungalow I had been slowly but surely (at least in my mind) restoring for a couple of years. Annie spread her grandmother's faded but pretty cherry-patterned tablecloth over our long, sturdy bois d'arc table. An old colleague, who taught industrial arts up at OSU in Stillwater, had painstakingly made the table for me in trade for one of my best paintings.

There was a pleasant breeze arriving from the North, picking up coolness as it crossed the Red River. Clara, Margaret, Annie and I joined hands, and I said the brief, and somewhat abrupt-sounding grace my paternal grandfather begrudgingly recited for his stern Methodist wife, my Grandma Alice. The lunch was top-notch, accompanied with the sound of our laughter and appreciative murmurs about the good food.

The girls, including Annie, had a way of talking gently about some things, in quiet tones I didn't always catch. It was as if they were sharing stories in code sometimes. I'd get the gist of bits, but suddenly there'd be a giggle or a hand-covered smile that I couldn't connect to the conversation. I didn't mind. There was a kindness to their tenor, a shared appreciation, an unhurried, delicate deference for each other.

It was a relatively cool ending for September. Summer had left early this year. Liz was already back in her dorm at Stephen F. Austin in Nacogdoches, getting an MS in forestry studies. A big fan of the East Texas loblolly pine, I'd let her plant three at various spots around the half acre the house stood on. It made her happy, and it always made me happy to watch her plant things with a contented demeanor that spoke of anticipation, of having a mind's-eye view of what the plant would grow into.

Liz was a level-headed achiever, and I rarely could help comparing her proudly to other parents' seemingly less level-headed daughters. Annie occasionally pointed out to me the possibility that other parents' daughters, like Clara and Margaret, might just be more relaxed and seemingly free-spirited around us exactly because we are not their parents! The girls removed dishes and bowls from the table into the kitchen, holding the screen door open for each other with elbows and toes. They thanked Annie for making lunch. "Awesome" one said. "Radical" said the other. A thought went through my mind that the girls might be taking some friendly jabs by using terms they assumed had originated with "our" generation.

I refilled mine and Annie's ice-tea glasses, and raised the pitcher aloft with a question mark, but the girls both smiled and shook their heads as they headed off to their equine wards.

Pickle and Tofu, upon hearing their owners' voices strolling towards them, awakened from their standing naps under the shade-canopy of an old post-oak tree near the round pen. Time for work.

Annie and I retired to the shaded patio, just off the back porch. We stretched out in the old cushion-covered wooden recliners, setting our glasses on the little wrought-iron glass-topped table between us. The horses had finished their naps. Now it was our turn. My sidekick quickly drifted off into that dreamy space between wake-world and sleep-world, hands folded across her faded denim skirt. Dappled bits of light fell through gaps in the shade cover of oak leaves high above us, creating a pattern of light and dark leaf-shapes across her starched white blouse.

One of my small mole-skin sketchbooks is never far away, so one rested on the table between us. A fine-tip Uniball ink pen was clipped to the elastic band that kept the book more or less securely closed. I raised myself to a sitting position as quietly as possible, facing dozing Annie from the side of my chair. There were many sketches and drawings of my beautiful sidekick in lots of sketchbooks over the last several years that we have been together. She's grown accustomed, and has learned that I sketch accurately with speed, so she doesn't feel like she's "posing," which is something Annie has little patience with, sadly. I filled the page-frame with her resting head, reclining torso and folded arms, suggesting just a bit of the structure of the Adirondack chair that hugged Annie's peaceful pose.

I liked the challenge of recording moments like this in ink lines. Ink forgives very little. My focus on form and contour and linear description has to be swift and correct, for the sketch to convey a sense of presence, not just convincing artifice. Finishing the sharp point on her shirt's right collar tip, following the line of her neck, my eyes came up to hers, unexpectedly wide-open, watching me draw. She was smiling at my concentration. Annie enjoys catching me unawares, sketching with furrowed brow, biting down on my lower lip.

Next day, after a truly windows-open, cool-breeze, fall night's sound sleep, we'd be sitting together on an ancient, creaking, oak-hewn pew at Elysia First Methodist for the Sunday Service. The long-dwindling, loyal congregation is always thrilled to see Annie, their favorite out-of-town visitor, not the least reason being that I will actually be present alongside her as well. Though raised a country Methodist, steeped in John Wesley rigor, my near-senior adult church attendance record has alarming gaps. That's how my Grandma Alice would put it.

From a corner of the front horse pasture, across the road from the round pen, Samson had watched much of the weekend training going on with Pickle, Tofu, and their teenage owners. He was occasionally joined by the old mare, Dolly, who was curious about what Samson was finding so interesting across the road. But she didn't linger long, being much more interested in the new crop of bright green winter rye as far as the eye could see. Solomon, my miniature donkey, had squeezed through the gate early that morning when I turned Samson and Dolly out to pasture, leaving the big white Pyrenees/Akbash mix to guard the sheep by himself. Caesar was more than up to the task, very clear about his duties, and confident of his skills.

Solomon seemed to have no concept of size. That is, I often figured that in his little head he saw himself the same size as his giant pal, Samson. The little guy would sometimes graze with such mindfulness that he would pass right under Samson's massive chest, long ear tips brushing Samson's belly as the miniature moved back and forth trying out this bit of grass and that. The gentle giant paid Solomon no mind, probably considering him on some days to be just a simple stable dog; a little companion to keep the equine star company on long trailer rides to shows and events, like the Fort Worth Livestock Show. Now and then, Solomon would maneuver his way into Samson's stall during evening feeding. He would stand beneath the big guy, gleaning whatever tasty oats might fall to the floor as Samson's big mouthfuls moved in and out of his feed bucket. It always amazed me that Samson never found fault with Sol's ears brushing against Sam's underside. I guess they were pals from the get-go.

Sol's expansive bray startles any person or animal within earshot. If too close, his sorrowful trumpet blast is quite painful. The little ass is also the smartest creature on the farm and can move with the silence of a viper when he wants to. Sol will always be the first to notice an unlatched gate or an open drum of alfalfa cubes. I once found him standing behind me in the kitchen. His efficient equine nose was stretched across the counter, sniffing at a closed breadbox. I had propped the screen door to the back porch open while I jostled a stack of several cardboard boxes of assorted groceries into the open kitchen. I never heard his tiny hooves tap-tapping gently up the wooden steps behind me. Sol was probably a stealthy international spy in another lifetime.

I plopped all the boxes on the center counter and turned to encounter a pest not normally seen in the kitchen. Facing me was the rear end of an uninvited four-legged guest. "What in the..." was the beginning of many a sworn epithet hurled in the direction of my

sometimes maddening, sometimes endearing, long-eared pal. A miniature Sicilian donkey, Sol's cuteness breaks all hearts of new visitors to
the farm. In reality, he is often simply a wolf in sheep's clothing, his
own little heart as mercenary as any Wall Street junk-bond mogul.

The tone of my invective spurred Sol into hasty retreat. With one
leap across the kitchen threshold onto the back-porch, and one more
over the back steps, he high-tailed it to safer pastures out back. I
unblocked the screen door and latched it shut for good measure. Even
without opposable thumbs, the little outlaw is quite skilled at
breaking and entering.

$\sim$

There's a daily rhythm at the farm, a pattern calculated by the
changing light of day, that humans and animals carry in their
heads. There's also a seasonal calendar carried in the memory
and tactile senses of each plant, mammal, fowl and bird, insect, fish,
and reptile on the farm. Every creature anticipates and experiences
each season's arrival, presence, and departure. Seeds, especially, are
atom-sized worlds of potential, waiting quietly for the correct convergence of time, light, soil, moisture, and temperature to prompt the
eruption in each of them, like low-murmuring microscopic volcanos.

Organic heirloom herb and produce seeds, like true wildflower
seeds, can be frustratingly ornery for impatient gardeners who want
their plants to follow orders. Engineered seeds—programmed eruption modules—are more predictable, therefore seem to be better little
soldiers. This can be a bit of an illusion, particularly flavor-wise.

The empirical evidence of wildflower seeds' apparent inconsis-
tency is proven by drivers' and passengers' visual observations as they
scan the landscape outside their mechanical module. For a couple of
years, for example, the same highway medians and perimeters are
bountiful in wildflower splendor. We put verbal exclamations marks
at the end of every sentence: "Wow!", "Oh my, look at *that!*" "I'm
speechless!"

Traveling the same route, a year later, the same annual anticipa-
tory travelers sigh with disappointment as they peer across mediocre

vistas, devoid of their shared memory of explosions of color stretching to the horizon. "Bummer," says one of the passenger teens. Wildflower seeds, in the wild, are the finest, most accurate timekeepers, the "Swiss movement" of natural watches. Waiting for the precise convergence of particular elements from nature's alchemy kit, wildflower seeds know when to awaken, and when to sleep. The seeds are not counting time according to our human eyes' entertainment needs.

The brilliant artist Chryssa played with this idea of the "presence" and "absence" of a thing to us. Viewers found themselves bewildered and delighted with her neon sculptures that would illuminate one set of colored letters, numbers, or shapes for a brief while, then extinguish those shapes while illuminating others in the same composition. Chryssa simply sped up the process of seasonal changes, of expectation and loss, of joy and longing. I go to a museum and see something that intrigues me, baffles me, or delights me. I remember certain aspects of the thing the next day, in my life away from the museum.

Days later, I want to return to see the thing again, to experience again those aspects that thrilled me before. To my surprise, I find something new, some aspect I hadn't noticed before, or realize that another aspect of the piece is not exactly as I "remembered" it. Chryssa is one of the best artists to look at who actually did a good job of examining the experience of time.

My parents were born on neighboring farms outside Irene, Texas. I was probably six or seven years old before it dawned on me that my cousins on both sides of the family were cousins only to me and not to each other. Strange, the "aha" moments of our childhood that stay significant to us for all our lives. My grandparents on both sides practiced what we now call "organic" gardening and farming. They never called it that, and certainly the word wasn't used in any context that I recall. The women in my family did occasionally use the word "organza" in conversations about fabrics and sewing. The word "organzine" defines the method for creating silk threads by twisting the silk fibers just so. The women in my family were all competent, and some expert, "seamstresses" to use the vernacular term of those days. They made clothes for each other, and when cash was tight, traded their skills for flour, canned goods, spices, and coffee.

Dad, and my uncles, did not practice organic farming. World War II veterans who returned to their Texas farming families after the war did not practice organic farming. Far from it, their generation celebrated "improved" fertilizers and feeds and "proven" herbicides and insecticides. The kinds of farming their own fathers had practiced required big families who even then could only farm so many acres themselves. Change was needed at all levels in agriculture, they thought. Modernization was required. Bigger yields, faster breeding, less maintenance; more control over nature's vagaries was a must. In fact, these vet farmers embraced, with open arms, DuPont's advertising slogan, first adopted in 1935: "Better things for better living through chemistry...."

All us cousins still pitched in and provided labor for each other's families to finish tilling on time, planting on time, fertilizing on time, weed and pest treating on time, picking on time. We teen boys sat on metal seats welded atop the distributor rigs. We hand-poured bagged herbicides and pesticides into canisters that spread the chemicals, as tractors pulled us up and down the rows. We never wore masks. Johnsongrass, however, was a formidable foe. It sprang up between rows of cotton and corn, according to my memory, overnight. I measured my own height's growth against that tall, ubiquitous, chemical-resistant weed, through all my teen years.

To sum up, my paternal granddad raised five kids, one son, and four daughters, on sixty-two acres of land, fertilized by manure and compost from those same acres. They lived on produce from their own garden, with plenty of potatoes and onions and greens for most of the year. He sold corn and cotton from those sixty-two acres. All four daughter's graduated from college, and later became teachers.

When I work in the garden today, repair a fence, gather eggs, or feel the weight of a lamb's body leaning against mine, organic farmer Grandad is with me. As a child, I was fascinated to watch him studying the calendar, his own seasonal journal notes, and the *Old Farmer's Almanac*. He'd make a decision, and then show me the date, explaining the reason for it. "Son," he would begin, "...we'll plant the seed potatoes on that date," touching the exact printed day with his finger. "The moon will be just right then." That seed-potato planting time in this part of Texas, by the way, still winds up being within just a couple of days of Valentine's Day.

Many of my cousins actually stayed in agriculture, farming some large acreage that they own, and leasing thousands of other acres. Corn, sorghum, maize, wheat, and cotton are the standards. They've gotten together with neighbors to buy regional cotton gins and opened a couple of their own feed and implement stores, just to stay in the game with modern ag consortiums and conglomerates managed by lawyers and investors in cities far away.

My broader farming family has been happier with me over the past few years, now that I have returned to that life myself. They are skeptical that my emphasis on organic heirloom herbs and produce will prove successful at market but realize that I'm funding my farm experiment startup with savings and retirement money. They regard my methods as esoteric, to say the least. One of my cousins, on a recent visit to see what I was up to, stretched up real tall and let out a long sigh before observing that, "Well, Sammy, all this just seems kind of *exotic* to me."

Teaching has always been regarded as a noble calling in my family. So I've had their respect for doing that these past couple of decades. Now, why anyone would actually take college classes in art, or more to the point, why art would be regarded as an actual *major*, is pretty much of a puzzle to them. God love them for it, but basically if there's not a cow or a barn in a painting, it's just not good art.

The first year I set up my tent at the historic farmer's market at Heritage Sqaure in Elysia, I spent a lot of time just educating folks about organic foods, no-till gardening, heirloom seeds, not to mention how to use herbs in cooking and canning. A well-known and successful tomato seller had the tent right across from me. After observing my rookie efforts over a couple of weekends, he came over for a chat. I keep an extra folding chair for such occasions.

My market neighbor introduced himself, then proceeded to give me his sound advice. And I appreciated that he meant well and was trying to be helpful.

"I've been at this"—he enveloped the whole acreage of the market within his broad gesture— "for a while. You're spending too much time talking with shoppers who aren't buying anything. You're not gonna make any money that way."

I replied, "Well, I guess it looks that way. But a lot of these folks just don't know anything about herbs, and some of our produce is just unfamiliar to them. I think they'll be back to try something new, after they've looked around."

"*Exactly,* Your stuff looks unfamiliar." He held up a pink and white striped eggplant whose ancestor seeds had been planted in French gardens in the fifteenth century. "And what does *heirloom* mean, by the way?" I explained, giving the usual lesson I provided for all, even for those shoppers "who aren't buying anything."

He held the beautiful eggplant out in the sun to observe its surface better. It glowed, like a Christmas tree ornament. He huffed a bit, then said quietly, so as not to be overheard "Well, the wife does like eggplant." He huffed again, and grudgingly bought some for her.

I was right, by the way, about return customers. One humorous little middle-aged lady was intrigued with the huge array of herbs in vases on display. She clutched her purse close against her breasts. Maybe she feared there might be purse-snatchers nearby. Or maybe she just liked having it at the ready. She amused Annie, who liked her instantly. A woman of few words, she would ask, "What's that?" while pointing at the salad burnet. I handed a stalk of the delicate, serrated leaf herb to her, suggesting she rub the leaf to release the scent. She did so, popping the stalk into her mouth, her eyes pointed upward, as she considered the aroma and flavor. "Cucumber!" she exclaimed with delight upon recognizing the taste. "Yes, Ma'am," I said with a big grin, happy for her to have discovered one of my favorite herbs in the garden. She asked about every herb on display. "What's that?" would be asked over and over, like a classic refrain of a Greek chorus. Annie thought it all wonderfully unique. I began to suspect that the tomato-seller might be correct about my spending too much time talking and not enough selling.

After an eternity of testing, the little woman smiled, pointing at the various items she wanted to purchase, and between somewhat pursed lips she would command "That. That. That. That...." She bought a hundred dollars' worth of herbs on her first visit.

Then, just like clockwork, she came every Saturday, and spent a hundred dollars in cash, simply by pointing. Words were no longer needed. We often wondered what she did with all those herbs. She admired our products, but had no interest in chatting, or even introductions. She bought with a purpose that went unknown to us forever.

I did a lot of fun research, like a new student, choosing the varieties of heirloom seeds to try out for my new organic herb and produce business. I wanted to sell uncommon items. I joined several national seed exchange organizations and firms. In particular, our lemon cucumbers were a big hit from the get-go. No one knew what they were, and none of our market customers had ever seen one. It's a lovely round yellow cucumber, just a tad smaller than a tennis ball. Included in a salad, the round slices look like ancient golden coins, providing a splendid color contrast to the greens of lettuce or spinach. The little round gems have a bright hint of lemon aftertaste. The first year we introduced the lemon cucumbers, a food writer for one of the big Dallas papers fell in love with them. For several years, she would mention us, alerting her readers that lemon cucumber season was near, and they would be available at our first timid little farmers market tent in Elysia.

$\sim$

There's a kind of matrix to the late summer and early fall in North Texas these days; it's hot all over, almost no rain, and most of us try to get the outside chores done in early morning and late evening. As in the movie *High Noon*, Barnes County folks are hiding in-doors at midday. They're not hiding indoors from a gang of outlaws arriving on the noon train. For that matter, there hasn't been any passenger train arriving in Elysia for many decades. County residents are indoors at noon simply to hide from the sun. On lawns in town, there's a repeated pattern of bright green rings of grass beneath trees, punctuated by surrounding seas of dying turf.

Trees across the region drop their leaves all at once, going dormant to preserve what water and nutrition is left inside. There will be lots of town lawns newly sodded at the first extended break in the drought. For farmers and ranchers, finding decent hay requires longer trips while pulling an eighteen-foot flatbed trailer. Calculating distance in diesel gallons is a depressing part of farming.

A common topic of discussion here in the country is water. The reality of the drought is very "up close and personal" for those of us in rural water co-ops. Friends and neighbors discuss methods of dealing with the drought. Gutters and rain-barrels have made a comeback, just in case a cloud may pass over your place.

During the droughts of the late fifties, Texas kids in town and country, were given frequent "spit baths," administered with a soapy washcloth and a little water. On Saturday nights, the family might share a galvanized round tub of the same soapy water, to luxuriate in individual standing baths.

A dear friend confided to us recently that she's taken to showering just every other day to help out. "Gray water" from kitchen sink or bathroom shower is popular again in town for potted plants.

If you have livestock or poultry, you ultimately become a convinced believer when it comes to electrolytes. The animals need them badly while suffering plenty of stress during recent exceedingly hot Texas summers. All our critters get dosed, either in oral gels or powders stirred into the drinking water. Yep, chickens especially. The word from vet and ag teacher friends is that this is the worst summer for poultry heat deaths in years. "Electrolyte 'em" is my advice.

Which reminds me of a recent summer with then young Solomon, my charming miniature Sicilian donkey, who got over-heated and blew his top. Well, to be honest, some of the charm had worn off fairly quickly during his early life at the farm. Because of his height, he's always felt he had the run of the place, as he can glide smoothly under the lowest pipe-fence available. Learning how to keep him out of everyone else's meal requires planning—and deception. Luring adolescent Sol to a secure spot for private dining, while the others ate their food in peace, took patience, cunning, and some cussing.

Early on, Solomon sometimes made the decision to act like an absolute ass at precisely the least helpful moment. A slow learner, it took him awhile to cotton on to his job as shepherd, the reason he was hired in the first place. "Enough, Sol!" I shouted angrily, as the little ornery equine chased yet another lamb across the creek and into the woods.

The sheep were stressed enough from the heat, so they could do without Sol's full-of-himself bullying. I got his halter from the tack room and hauled him post-haste into isolation (the unused goat pen) for disrupting the peace.

Actually, I did sympathize with the little donkey. For weeks he'd served faithfully as baby-sitter and companion for Blaze, the five-month-old orange colt. Penned up with the baby, eating and sleeping with the frisky youngster, and tolerating his immaturity, the older equine was surely fed up. Sol must have been thinking "Why me?! I'm almost a year and a half old!" The "tough love" required to wean a colt from his momma is greatly facilitated by the companionship of a good-natured, hail-fellow-well-met like Solomon. The unfairness of the punishment was written all over the little guy's tragic donkey face, as he peered through the rails of his goat-pen prison, watching Blaze move freely about the barnyard.

An old artist friend from Baltimore was visiting for a few days during that livestock dust up. And of course she thought Sol hung the moon. (Who wouldn't?) She phoned for a chat after returning to her urban loft up north. Her first requested update was about the juvenile delinquent donkey. "So, has precious Solomon survived his unde-served time out?" Well put.

Early October in North Texas always sounds cooler than it ever is. The leaves in the trees are brown or yellow from sheer heat exhaus-tion. During my first year in Grand Forks, North Dakota, early October days were in the mid-fifties. It was heaven. Being a Texas boy, newly stationed at the nearby big Strategic Air Command (SAC) Base, I could not anticipate the hell of winter that was approaching. Grand Forks is a lovely college town, situated on the Red River of the North, dividing North Dakota and Minnesota. All the trees in North Dakota live in Grand Forks, lined along both sides of the Red River. Everything else was wheat, sugar beets, or potatoes, as far as the eye can see. That's for about three months. From November to early

June, back then, the landscape was blurred by nine months of horizontal snow, blowing straight down out of Winnipeg, Manitoba.

On a still and blistering hot North Texas early October day at the farm, snow sounded refreshing. The air had no movement, just a penetrating heat. At midday, the free-ranging chickens were mostly huddled in clusters here and there around the yard, seeking whatever bits of shade could be found under this or that bush and cedar.

The chickens had stopped laying, as always, in the closing days of a hot summer. During this seasonal molting time, even the faithful Rhode Island Reds will join the annual strike. Once a year, almost like clockwork, I can count on the farm's poultry labor force implementing a planned work stoppage. This annual mutiny always left management wringing hands and scratching heads. "Is it permanent?" "What about our customers?"

We ask such questions as we carefully observe every move of our winged employees. This one seems to be off by herself more, that one seems thinner. Is she limping? Do they need more electrolytes? Such intense analysis of fowl behavior, of course, can have diminishing returns. I mean, there's only so much you can learn from watching one chicken peck at hen-scratch and oyster shell-crush.

Old-time chicken farmers advise various solutions. "Give 'em some watermelon." Ours seem to prefer the large Black Diamond, by the way. I suspect they get a kick out of seeing us struggle under the weight of one of those giant beauties. I still grow a small patch of Black Diamonds just for the farm, but now just take Moon and Stars or Blacktail Mountain watermelons to market. They're usually about ten pounds. Most farmers' market customers don't want to hand-carry a fifty-pound Black Diamond around.

One neighbor said they had researched the internet and come up with the idea to try cat food, as an appetite stimulant. Well, we're usually pretty much open to trying unorthodox ag remedies up at the farm but were worried about the probable inclusion of animal protein in some cat food, maybe even chicken by-products, so we didn't try that one. "Tomatoes will do the trick. Chickens like acid." suggested another neighbor.

Our girls especially liked Matt's Wild Cherry, a precious berry-sized gem I unwisely introduced at market one summer. These tiny tomatoes are always a delightful surprise for dinner guests, when a handful is tossed into the pot at the last minute prior to serving anything with marinara sauce. They're little bombs of flavor. Naturally, our farm fowl preferred the most difficult-to-harvest product from our organic gardens. We have picky chickens.

I was amused recently at a sight on my way to the barn. Robin, a new high school helper, had dutifully plopped a very large watermelon down in the middle of the sweltering barn yard, a treat for the nearby free-ranging hens. She stood sternly erect above her charges, arms crossed, waiting to measure their feathered response to the gift.

The melon had burst in a big radial pattern. Instantly, from nowhere it seemed, a livestock huddle formed, jostling farmhand Robin for position. Joining in on the melon feast were Sol, the donkey, Blaze, the orange colt, two of the fat-tailed, red Tunis lambs, assembled chickens and guineas, all attracted to the barnyard buffet.

To add to this fraternal gathering, the late summer's crop of barn-kittens frolicked, wrestled, and rolled over each other amongst the banquet, beneath the assorted legs of other critter-species, the little cats apparently not as hungry (or polite) as the undisturbed adult animal guests.

For all appearances, it might have been the first (animal) Thanksgiving. It was like a living-tableau presentation of Edward Hicks' *The Peaceable Kingdom*. Edward Hicks (1780-1849) painted about a hundred illustrations of his wonderful Quaker vision: two-legged and four-legged creatures of all sorts, suspended in a moment of calm co-existence, against a background of earth's verdant foliage.

Domestic animals resting peacefully with wild animals, that was Hicks' vision. Even the occasional child drapes a chubby arm safely over the neck of an awake lion. Adult figures are often depicted at a distance, quietly observing the pastoral allegory, as if attending a Sunday school lesson on the verses of Isaiah 11: 6-9.

The subject reflects the artist's passionate interests in religion, nature, and farming. Hicks was a Quaker minister, whose sermons were very popular. He earned a living selling many versions of *The Peaceable Kingdom*, and by painting elaborate signs, furniture, and coaches. He tried farming for a while but made better money lettering signs.

Maybe Edward Hicks should have included barn-cats and chickens in more of his pictures. After all, he was depicting American barnyards and rural settings. Regarding the chickens in our own little peaceable kingdom, I really don't want folks to get the idea that management is unresponsive to the needs of our poultry workers.

Our poultry is, well, pampered. The yard foreman, Clara, has several of her favorites trained. I guess to a horse trainer, getting chickens to do tricks is relatively easy. And of course her favorites are named. Lucy, a Rhode Island Red, will leap up into our arms and immediately take a nap. Ivory, a Barred Rock, will fly up onto the rim of any bucket being transported, and she will perch there forever while her masters walk around the barn yard doing chores. Personally, I think Ivory is just hitching a free ride.

Art students came to the farm the other day. It's always exciting to them, and I enjoy it too.

Suzie, my old friend and colleague at the Barnes County Community College, brings a busload of art majors for a day of sketching in the country with "Sam the Farmer" (me). She brings them in the fall, and again in the spring, bookending the hottest and coldest parts of the year.

Sometimes the art department is able to use the two relatively new air-conditioned vans recently purchased by the county. This fall, they came in the old battered yellow Bluebird bus inherited years ago from the Audie Murphy High School near the college campus. Their donkeys were secured to the roof of the old bus with a motley assortment of bungee cords and tie-downs.

Let me explain the "donkeys" on the roof of the bus. Drawing benches are universal furniture used throughout the US, the UK, and Europe. The basic structure is almost always the same form, constructed of three sides, two legs and an extended bench-seat. One leg rises about a foot above the end of the seat. Each of the three "planks," or sides, is about two feet by thirteen inches. The seat is usually about thirty inches long and includes a short ledge at the tall end to serve as a base of support for drawing boards. Drawing boards are usually large enough to hold an eighteen-by-twenty-four-inch drawing pad and normally have securing clamps on one of the short sides.

Years ago, I had a teacher exchange year as an art lecturer at a small college in Derbyshire, UK. My Brit students all referred to the drawing benches as "donkeys." I brought the term home with me, and it became the standard name in the art department.

The Barnes County art students are always delighted that sketching and drawing at my farm includes the presence of a live donkey; a curious one, at that, who will occasionally pause at a student's drawing, observe, and tilt his long ears at forty-five degrees, as if doing a silent critique of the work. Solomon has been known to blare out with his loudest bugle-braying on occasion, startling the young artist to fall off of their own wooden donkey.

Susie is a good teacher. I hired her years ago when I reluctantly agreed to be department coordinator, and so was supervisor to adjunct drawing and painting faculty. I enjoyed the camaraderie with the younger teachers but loathed the administrative mandates that seemed to be in a perpetual repeat cycle of wheel-spinning. It's fun to have Suzie at the farm. As she instructs and cajoles the students, her words are sometimes like listening to myself. She likes coming to the farm and appreciates that the students are getting twice their money's worth, being taught by two artist teachers who themselves draw and sketch outdoors whenever possible.

I preselect promising views for her wards, often depending on what the natural props within various landscape views are offering in a seasonal sense; that is, for example, will the grass beyond that fence rail be tall during a particular field day, or have been eaten to the base by the horses? Will this or that tree have branches obscured by fat, brightly colored orange and yellow and red leaves, or just starting to show the promise of summer with profusions of small, round bright green leaves, with limbs and branches that stand out like heavy ink lines?

I love drawing landscapes, and I love teaching students how to do it. As with any drawing, for beginners, one of the hardest things to understand is that they must spend as much time *seeing* their subject as drawing it. First-time students often expect that the teacher is going to begin the class by teaching them trade secrets, like "This is how we draw a tree," or "This is how we draw a cloud, a flower, or a dog named Fido." The students had unharnessed their donkeys from the roof of the bus, passing them down, fire-brigade style. They had gathered their toolboxes, tablets, viewfinders and Masonite drawing boards. They stood in contrapposto poses, first on this foot, then the other, impatient to get started. The morning sun was rising, so hats and caps were being adjusted, along with last-minute applications of bug spray and sunscreen. Some students had plopped astride their donkeys, tired of standing on the pea-gravel parking area.

Suzie and I had already gone over the location of views I had chosen. She was familiar with all, of course, and understood that the selection was driven by seasonal considerations. She had already divided the twenty students into groups of five. She would lead her two groups to their sites, and I would do the same, wooden donkeys at hips for all.

She led her groups toward views that looked over an old narrow creek with cattails and overhanging, drooping branches of an ancient cottonwood tree. The seeds for that huge cottonwood had likely been deposited 150 years ago by a scissortail on the eastern range of his flightpath that originated over Quanah Parker's hunting grounds in West Texas.

One of her groups would face northwest and the other southwest.

Suzie carefully looked at each student's eye-level view, herself astride their donkey, in order to help each make adjustments to maximize a view that contained obvious foreground, middle-ground, and background shapes and spaces. The creek itself became a strong diagonal device for illusion of depth perspective in either the northwest or southwest direction. The students were learning practical application of *atmospheric perspective* drawing elements.

For my two groups, those facing southeast saw within their viewfinders (a ten-by-twelve-inch cut matboard that framed their views) a young crape myrtle in the foreground, a three-sided covered wooden windbreak for the sheep on brisk days, and a pond with a few mesquite trees on the far side.

The dirt road crossed the middle ground view at a diagonal, leading the eye to the pond in the background. The other group, further along the road, faced SW with a picnic table in the foreground, half of the round pen in the middle ground and a grove of post oaks in the background. A well-worn foot path provided a curving line, in the students' viewfinder's rectangular "window," that receded across the meadow into the grove.

So, for all the students, the sun was at their backs, and now the landscape lesson began.

We drew until noon. Suzie had ordered box lunches for everybody. The college was so old-fashioned the board of directors still funded an actual cafeteria with a live staff. The box lunches were individual orders: this one, vegan; that one, extra jalapeno; the next, with blackened, not fried, tilapia tacos, and so on. It gave one hope that Barnes County could keep the ubiquitous, sub-contracted, fast-food franchise mania at bay a little longer.

The students left their donkeys in exactly the same position, to return to the same view after lunch. Also after lunch, I'd give all of them my short lecture on how fast the earth is turning, so they will observe how different the afternoon sun and shade is compared with the morning. The objects in their viewfinders are in their same places, but much of the tonality of the space will have changed completely. It helps the art students to consider, and appreciate, how precious were the few moments available each day of the same light, say, for the Dutch Master Vermeer to illuminate his models. It kind of explains why the artist only painted forty pictures in a lifetime.

For the afternoon drawing session, Susie and I switched places, so that each group of student artists spent time with a different artist-teacher. As I moved from student to student, I made small adjustments to their drawings when needed, or illustrated a helpful technique by demonstrating a suggested type of blending values or reducing textural detail in the middle ground and the like.

On a couple of the landscapes, I had the whole group gather around as I gave mini critiques of the drawings, pointing out what was working best in the selected example, and what needed improving.

During my study of the afternoon group's efforts, I was reminded of Suzie's younger teaching method. She'd advised the students to take a cellphone photo of their chosen view, just to record the position of the shadow and light in the scene at that preferred moment. Sometimes I'm a slow learner regarding technology. Sometimes I'm even a neo-Luddite, for that matter.

The sun was heavy, falling toward the horizon. We had the students line all the easels beside each other creating a continuous wall of support for the eighteen-by-twenty-four-inch drawing boards. Group critiques are rich experiences for all concerned. The class gets to see twenty or so individual drawings attempting to achieve the same goal, a convincing illusion of actual three-dimensional landscape space on a flat, two-dimensional piece of paper. The contents of the subject are alike, but each drawing has its own individual view. Landscape drawings seen in a row, always suggest a kind of panoramic movement, very cinematic.

The group critique is probably my favorite classroom event, conducted during decades of my teaching career. Students are asked to discuss each other's works, using the manner modeled by their instructors; in this case, me and Suzie. Students know to comment on something they see that is working well toward a specific objective, such as leading the viewer's eye effectively into the background or maintaining a wide variety of lights and darks across the page. Then to look for areas that need adjustment, or that seem unfinished (which is usually the case). Students learn not only from talking with each other about the lesson's meaning, but mostly they learn from carefully *seeing* twenty visual solutions to the same lesson.

The students, having secured their own donkeys back atop the old yellow bus, climb aboard by ones and twos. They shake my hand. Some give me a hug. They all pat long-eared Sol on the head or scratch his withers. He stands proudly next to me, as if he's hosted the whole day's affair. Suzie boards last, beaming at me with appreciation for another successful field trip. Life is a wheel. Student and teacher part again, until the next season's landscape lesson.

∾

T he fall garden refreshes the mind and the body. The ancient Greeks would have approved of that grateful acknowledge-ment. Even under full sun shining warm and bright, cooling breezes seem ever cooler beneath the shade of a broad-brimmed straw hat. Mornings are especially pleasant reminders that intense summer heat in the garden will not return for over nine months. The very air around us seems to breathe a sigh of relief.

Were we actual vendors in ancient Athens' *agora*, or at our own local farmers' *mercatus* in Rome's busy Forum, we'd be selling much the same herbs and produce then as now. Cato's *De Agri Cultura*, also known as *On Farming* or *On Agriculture* is, in part, a kind of farmer's manual, or almanac, to be shared with farm neighbors. Dated about 160 B.C., Cato's tome praises farming as a noble vocation. The work was of significant influence on Roman Emperor Augustus (63 B.C. to A.D. 14), who wisely promoted and marketed Roman farm exports worldwide. Augustus' commercial aims for Rome's international agri-cultural success precede Austin's own GO TEXAN hopes by a few centuries.

Cato's work is considered by many to also be the first cookbook, as it includes many farm recipes. One chapter praises the homeopathic attributes of cabbage; in particular, its effectiveness as a hangover remedy. I imagine this chapter was often consulted by Roman merry-makers. Leaving their summer togas at home, many of our current urban customers have been arriving early mornings at market wearing sweaters. That's a sight we haven't seen, for, well, about nine months. Hmmm, earth's natural cycle has a familiar ring to it, doesn't it?

We've been at the Farmers Market in Elysia's Heritage Square every Saturday since April. It's a lovely public space, canopied by a half-acre of tall shade provided by hundred-year-old pecans, planted by the town's founders. Several Saturdays this summer were real scorchers, anywhere in Barnes County, so vendors and customers at Heritage Square were thankful for good town planning.

I'll be folding the tent on the farmers market the last Saturday in October, returning next April. For the rest of fall, into winter, we will continue regular Friday deliveries of our organic herbs and produce to several chefs in Fort Worth and Dallas. Word travels fast, and area chefs sent scouts (their sous chefs) in our very first year at market to see what Bartlett Farm had to offer.

There are a number of surprises just now in the Fall garden. Cherry-husk tomatoes (also known as ground-cherries) are beautiful little globes of flavor wrapped in a paper-thin shell. When ripe, the fruit is shiny yellow and has a uniquely sweet and tart flavor all its own. My first fall crop was a total surprise, the gift of a passing bird who had most likely stopped off to dine at one of my trial seed beds near the back patio of the house. The unintended presence of the cherry-husks was irritating to me when I initially saw them sprawling happily across a bed of freshly sprouting leafy green lettuce. But I was impressed with the plant's tenacious insistence to propagate wherever soil existed, regardless of prior tenants. The cherry-husk tomato plant grows low to the ground, with big fat leaves that spread faster than new concrete can be poured over "undeveloped" Texas farmland.

The crowded lettuce family is now evicted and will be moved to more advantageous climes. A new exotic boarder will occupy that bed. Practicing organic, no-till and raised-bed, sustainable gardening requires adjustments. Living things like to grow in such rich and healthy dirt, sometimes unplanned or unwanted things. As my old staff sergeant supervisor in the Air Force print shop used to say during unexpectedly difficult times, "make like a willow and bend with the breeze."

Building a raised bed frame does involve serious effort, and can be a pricey investment, initially. However, the resultant productivity, ease of planting, maintenance and harvesting will reward your labor ten-fold the first season. Weed control, alone, in a raised bed, becomes therapeutic achievement. The framed definition of workspace in a raised box is great incentive toward a sense of task completion.

Fighting nature with pesticides and chemical-based fertilizers only wins you temporary victories, with bigger battles down the road. Imposing uncompromising obedience to your master plan or design upon natural, growing things is never a winning proposition. There are organic alternatives to commercial pesticides and herbicides. For example, we keep a fifty-five-gallon drum of 20 percent vinegar handy for use on unwanted grass, weeds, and fire ants. Spray the vinegar directly on weedy or grassy areas that are starting to encroach too close to crops. For fire ant control, pour the vinegar like pancake syrup around the mound, from top to bottom. Mind you, 20 percent vinegar will kill any plant within a foot's radius of application, but it is organic and will leach away from the targeted soil in about a week.

Whatever you do in the way of garden maintenance, there's always some rude opportunist waiting, just below the surface, to pop up and say, "Howdy, cousin!" to the dismay of your desired plant residents. It's just a lot easier to spot the random intruder in a raised bed.

Back when I had first moved to the country, taking my artist hands to farming, I was enjoying a splendid November evening's reverie near the then small, makeshift, chicken yard. Tall orange and pink and yellow clouds stretched across the western sky's landscape, from Fort Worth in the south to Ardmore, Oklahoma, in the north. The meditative moment was irreverently interrupted, though that's not an unusual occurrence in the country, by the way. I dropped the toolkit from one hand, a cold can of beer from the other, and my lower jaw, at the sight of my orange colt, Blaze, and his older pal, Solomon, the little miniature Sicilian donkey, trespassing inside the chicken coop! There they were, after all I'd done for them, literally scrounging around for chicken feed. The two equine bandits had managed to wiggle their fat bodies through the narrow, but poorly secured screen-door of the tiny chicken yard and coop.

These two young farm-slackers would like me to think them nutritionally deprived, even to the point of pity. But Solomon's too-round belly belies him having missed any meals. Infant colt Blaze follows tiny Sol's every lead, so hasn't any idea that in less than a year, there's no way his own future big quarter horse butt will be able to pass through the chicken coop door again.

Sol, the miniature, of course has reached his full potential height. He was hoping, I'm sure, to make it to an expected thirty inches tall, but no luck yet. Now two years old, all that's left for Sol is hope. Well, his Napoleonic confidence will probably always overcome any obstacle, especially when he has really important horses like Blaze following his every devious directive. The orange colt doesn't equate Sol's smaller size to be representative of anything significant, but somehow Blaze knows that Sol is older. So, the young colt is often led down the wrong (and narrow) path by the cunning ass, his elder.

The orange sun was setting over the neighbor's barn, distracting me from chores. The sky was streaked with bright pink, paint-brush-like strokes, glazed over with orange and yellow layers, aping Thomas Moran landscapes at the Gilcrease Museum in Tulsa. Stars already appeared in the dark, navy-blue sky above. A single, thread-like line of pale powder-blue could be seen just above the horizon, the last of daylight's evidence waning. It looked like a thin, celestial Navajo turquoise-bead necklace, in the near, night heavens, stretching up over the distant Ouachita Mountains to the north.

The painter in me wanted to linger, to soak in nature's finest sky art, but reality brought me back down to North Texas earth. As warden of my livestock menagerie, I had fences to mend, literally.

It was a cold evening already, with a hard freeze coming overnight. I stepped into the crowded, but still mostly fenced-in chicken-yard, rounded up the little wannabe mustangs, and escorted them back into the barnyard. Immediately both equine heads were in the hen-feed bucket I'd carelessly left by the yard door. All critters love chicken feed for some reason. The corn, I guess.

I shushed the boys away and shook the bucket so the "free range" chickens would hear the grain, while calling them to roost for the night. They weren't far away, having been hovering near the coop, just waiting for the four-legged bullies to exit their little protected poultry cloister. The chickens followed me, and the bucket, into their yard, to enjoy a snack and then climb the cedar ladder up to their roost to settle in for a cold night. I'd certainly have the heat lamp on for them later, what with the night's forecast.

The look I was going for in the design of the chicken coop, by the way, was sort of a cross between a Green Acres TV show shed and an A-frame Swiss chalet. It was a hodge-podge of re-purposed materials, including rusty corrugated tin, spare plywood, and scrap cedar boards. The hens seemed to approve of their home, eager to turn in after a hard day's free ranging. The empty feed bucket became a full egg bucket at day's end. I moved the day-time doorstop (a brick) from the bottom edge of the old wooden screen-door and wound a worn bungee cord tightly across the whole patchwork portal, hoping at last that I'd finally secured the tired, tucked-winged assembly in for the night.

I originally took great pains with the construction of the chicken yard, burying the chicken-wire in a foot-deep trench, and even extending a continuous wire ceiling over the whole top of the yard, not unlike traditional, draping circus-tent structures. An aged over-hanging cedar tree, trimmed of lower limbs up to about eight feet, provided lots of stiff branches as support for the assorted colorful bungee cords I attached to hold up the chicken wire canopy.

It was a pain to complete, but I was able to smile with relief as I closed the last gap in the free-form chicken-wire cover over the yard. No night-hunting critters would be able to climb over the wall and into the chicken coop.

The waning evening light was darker, still, beneath the shade of the tall old cedar tree that served as the center pole to my ersatz chicken-yard circus-tent. Suddenly, a great horned owl swooped right over our heads (mine and the chickens). The handsome, floating creature glided silently only a few inches above, arrogantly peering into the wire-canopy enclosure, no doubt with plans of upcoming poultry meals at my expense.

Modern flying drones are meager terrain and temperature calculators, when compared to the computational and analytical eyes and ears of a winged winter visitor, like the owl. With all its sensory nerves and muscles and tissue responding to those time-proven sound and sight messages, such an adept hunter usually finds a way to outsmart farmers.

Majestic owls and hawks always provoke a respectful sense of awe in us wingless beings, but we like them better without valuable egg-layers in their talons. And, of course, I didn't let any of the chicks free-range in the daytime until they had become much larger and heavier talon-targets.

Guard your chickens.

❧

Nike, the warrior pup, proved to me early on that she was taking no guff from the older resident farm dogs. Plus, like her namesake, she was a beauty. After a good towel rub-down, she literally leapt into her coat one chill-to-the-bone November evening. The very long, nine-month-old Bluetick coonhound greeted me just inside the front gate, tail-wagging, soaked, and eager to "load up" into the truck for the short but warm ride up to the barn. Her pal, Blackie, was nowhere to be seen, but would surely follow along shortly, after dispatching some careless vole or field mouse.

I had stayed in town longer than expected, waiting at the feed-store for late delivery of a new box of water filter canisters. My customers like it that I irrigate my herbs and produce with water free of chlorine and unnecessary metals. Penny, co-owner of the store, kindly brought me a cup of coffee from the office, which I was enjoying as I leaned on the front countertop, watching her husband, Pete, deal with a dilemma. He was scratching his bald head while trying to figure out the assembly instructions for a new DIY hotwire solar charger, which he now had spread out in a jumble of assorted parts on the counter. I moved my coffee cup away from the expanding conflagration.

I noticed Bert outside, one of the afterschool helpers, moving three bags of alfalfa cubes from the truck bed to the backseat of my crew cab. Diagonal rainfall had begun from the northwest. I gave him a thumbs-up thank you as he ran for cover. The wavy glass in the old front doors was frosting over. A blue norther had blown in suddenly, as they always do. I told Pete I'd come back tomorrow, and thanks for the coffee.

The old cowbell hanging on the front door clanged loudly as I left. I felt sleet pellets along with the rain as I climbed into the truck. Snow joined in, forming cold white diagonal lines in the dark ahead, as I carefully maneuvered the many slick curves of the county road back to the farm.

Nike was wet to the bone, which isn't hard to do as her hide is so thin. Well-intentioned neighbors and friends chat with her when she accompanies me to our rural filling station or to Pete's feed store in Elysia. They are prone to ask, "Is that dog gettin' enough to eat?"

She's an attractive hound and everybody wants to take care of her. Pete, of all her fans, knows the hound is getting fed plenty, as he buys new horses for his wife Penny just off my dog food bill.

The black-and-white pup's rib-bones were chattering against each other (she does this to exaggerate her plight on any cold day). We pulled up in front of the west end of the barn. The instant I opened my door of the truck, Nike flew across my lap and was standing at the double doors of the barn, her long black nose pressed into the thin gap between. She was ready to don her favorite warm coat for the night.

It was snowing buckets already at the farm. My drive back from restaurant deliveries to downtown Fort Worth earlier that day was shared by some race-car drivers speeding up US 287 through bits of occasional mist. I was just hoping to get home now from Elysia before the forecasted snow started falling. I could tell from the size of the big, cold and sluggish raindrops on my windshield that they were doing a good job of turning to snow very soon.

Being stationed at Grand Forks AFB, North Dakota, as I was for a few years, will teach you a lot about snow. I pulled the main barn doors apart enough for Nike and me to tumble into the wide hall of the barn, out of the cold. She raced to the foot of a sturdy easel I had downstairs for repairs, wagging her long, cold tail as she peered up toward her new winter coat. It hung from the top of the easel, where I had placed it early in the morning before letting her out for the day's adventures. It is a handsome coat.

It's not really a dog coat. It's a foal's coat. Nike's long frame could never tuck itself into a meager dog's coat. It's black and white, in a striking design of simple geometric white lines on a black base. It looks great on the hound's black and white spotted hide. I'd picked it out at Horse and Rider, the local house of fashion. The neck is shearling-lined, of which Nike is particularly proud. She enjoys the procedure required to attach all the clips and adjust the cross-straps, just as she's seen me do a thousand times when putting on the horses' coats for winter. Maybe she really thinks she's a horse.

Blackie's already curled up on her bed up against the hall closet. She is a hardworking farm dog and ready to turn in when the sun starts down over the hill. Nike, on the other hand, is a hound. Like Murph, my old Bluetick, rest his soul, Nike would prefer to stay up all night, chasing animals (real and imagined) into trees and through creek-beds. Coonhounds love the morbid sound of their own distinctive voices, especially at night. I don't recommend this breed for urban dwellers.

Nike struts right up the hall to the closed barn door, rubbing up against the cedar boards to feel the warm texture of the thick coat against her thin skin. She glances back at me pitifully, whining a little, pleading for me to let her outside for a night of partying now that she's dressed for the cold. I squat beside Blackie, stroking her silky, sleepy head. "Nike, come here." I say gently, while pointing to her bed next to Blackie's. The nine-month-old spotted-pup gives up her futile petition to go wandering afar in the dark, wags her tail, and steps lively over for some petting.

Nike makes three sleek circles on her cushy bed before plopping down to sleep beside her mongrel pal. Her turning gesture makes me recall the melody and refrain of Elder Joseph Brackett's peaceful song, the old Shaker hymn *Simple Gifts*.

> *'Tis the gift to be simple, 'tis the gift to be free*
> *'Tis the gift to come down where we ought to be,*
> *And when we find ourselves in the place just right,*
> *'Twill be in the valley of love and delight.*
> *When true simplicity is gain'd,*
> *To bow and to bend we shan't be asham'd,*
> *To turn, turn will be our delight,*
> *Till by turning, turning we come 'round right.*

Murph, the Bluetick Coonhound

TWO

Winter Coats

Watching snow fall heavily outside the farm office window has helped distract me from the bad cold I've had for a couple of days. Even with a stuffed head, the rare snowfall is pleasant to watch. Snow evokes memories of sledding or making snowmen with childhood friends and cousins. Perhaps because central Texas youngsters didn't get to see the magical white stuff often, it resides in a part of the brain that stores pleasant recall.

Other memories of snow are denser, more like an avalanche. At Grand Forks AFB, snow was our constant companion for all the years I spent there. The snow blew horizontally, with a ferocity that kept all human figures leaning on the diagonal. Humans were able to stand vertically in North Dakota only from mid-June to mid-August. The biggest snowflakes up there are in early May each year. Big, fat, wet, near snow-ball size things that hit you with a "smack!" Wind in North Dakota rages across Manitoba on a mad pace which must maintain its fury long enough to reach Kansas, dragging as much snow with it as possible. Sometimes Oklahoma and North Texas get the tail end of such storms, still formidable.

As I recall, except along the Red River of the North, North

Dakota and environs is not simply flat, it is treeless. The horizon extends 360 degrees around you into infinity, all at the exact same level, with an uninterrupted view. The soil is rich. North Dakota is the bottom of a huge prehistoric body of water. The land sleeps nine months of the year under a thick blanket of white. In the summer, some big farms get in two crops by working the land twenty-four hours a day. Being a Texas boy, I was amazed at the endless lines of railcars moving beside highways, between the giant fields, laden with fat sugar-beets, red wheat, potatoes, or flax.

Live a couple of winters up in the Dakotas region and you soon learn the meaning of the word "whiteout." Being indoors during a Nodak (what North Dakotans call themselves) snowstorm is not for coziness, it's about survival. Work is different in conditions like that, of course. I was a printer in the Air Force, so I enjoyed a warm setting, watching the day's blizzard blow past the window, my coffee cup within arm's reach of my press.

For extra money, I worked part-time jobs for Grand Forks Superior Feed and Seed Company and for various farmers in the area. Moving eighty-pound bags of red wheat seed all day was monotonous, but the money was good for uneducated labor. Working for farmers out on the prairie was more interesting. They did things differently up there, compared with the methods of my Texas farming family. For one thing, with the exception of mid-July, heavy coats and parkas were at the ready all year.

I loaded hay one summer for a friend's dad at a farm between Grand Forks and Fargo (to the south). The barns were so big and tall, we used a cherry-picker to stack the hay. At another farm, lambing season was an all indoors affair. As a serious blizzard roared outside, lambs were dropping all over the place at once. The whole operation took place in an endless array of pens inside a series of buildings that would have covered several city blocks. This was serious, mass lambing, with numbing bleating decibels never heard even at the busy Fort Worth Junior Livestock Show.

Working at the feed and seed company in Grand Forks gave me a perspective on how the bigger, richer grain and produce outfits survived the snow. Those wealthy farming families toughed out the winters from the vantage point of a Florida beach, or "The Valley" of Texas, amongst ruby red grapefruit groves and sunshine. One of the largest family concerns that bought literally tons of feed and seed per week painted all their farm trucks and cars the same dark green color. I asked about the practice, knowing that all that dark metal would get plenty hot in the sun back home.

My co-workers looked at me as if I was crazy.

"What's the color of most vehicles down your way, Tex?" one older fellow asked, as he tossed up a bag of wheat seed to me as if it were a loaf of bread. I thought a moment. "White or tan, mostly, I guess" was my answer. "Well, son, that don't work up here."

At some point during my four-year stay in the print shop at Grand Forks AFB, on annual regular leave home to Texas, I bought a car suitable for Nodak winters. It was a used two-door Rambler American, with a straight six motor that would accept a tank heater. With the help of an industrial-rated extension cord, I could keep the block warm all winter. I paid six hundred dollars for it at a used-car dealership on Jefferson Street in Oak Cliff. It never failed me for the rest of my tour. Sadly, the little car was white, so it was often invisible.

I've had a number of Bluetick Coonhounds over the years. There's a distinct sense of *gravitas* in their gaze that always makes me think there must be an old soul inside that noble head. My boon companion Murph preceded Nike, and her sweet persona prompts fond memories of adventures with the old fellow, rest in peace.

Murph raised an elegant black-and-white spotted, long-nosed head off of his bony, crossed front legs. He slowly opened his sad, coonhound eyes to observe what all of the ruckus was about in the barnyard. Despite the thick, pancake-like flaps that hung heavily over his ear canals, Murph could hear anything that made a noise, regardless of decibel. He yawned, in no big hurry to inquire about the current disturbance, recognizing it as simply a spat amongst domestic, coddled animals. Only wildlife could drive Murph crazy enough to want to climb a tree.

The long, thin, spotted canine had been dreaming a wonderful, rewarding dream; thus his relaxed, even nonchalant, return to real life scenes. The possibility of hunger, discomfort, or a kick from one of the larger farm animals was so much in the very distant periphery of his memory that he woke up peacefully, as a man who had never been to war.

Murph had been dreaming that he was Master of Hackberry Creek. His lean, handsome Dog Dukeness stood atop the Bartlett Farm dam which had created a one-acre lake on the northeast side of the farm. A large drainpipe just a few feet below the dam's ridge provided run-off of excess lake water into the faithful creek. In Murph's dream, it was springtime.

Unusually strong Autumn rains had pummeled the farm, just outside the bucolic town of Elysia. (The original settlement was named by founders who regarded themselves as modern aspirant Athenians). In Murph's dreams, floods were floods, period, and forever. Sun was sun...forever. (No global warming or climate change variations entered his coonhound dreams). For the length of the dog's dream, all time and experience were constant. Whatever he dreamed existed only then within his sleeping mind. The hound didn't remember dreams, only scents.

Reality required a lot from Murph. Prior to finding me, the young hound had wandered in the wilderness for a long time. Hungry, cold, and in constant danger of being shot in the rear-end repeatedly by lazy hunters who wanted him to be more enthusiastic during the chase. He could hear the hunters behind him say things like "Hell! Shoot that lazy coon-dog again in the ass! Make him hunt!" He was being trained to hunt by men with no classical aspirations.

As I would soon learn from our local vet, reality was that Murph had three large metal pellets (not little BBs) in his rear, fired from high-velocity pellet pistols. One was so close to the spine it is a miracle the hound wasn't crippled. The push-pin shaped pellets floated around his skinny spine's bottom bones all the time he belonged to me.

The hound, of course, was ignorant of empirical science, cause and effect, climate-change, and the like, so he just woke up slowly, without much complaint. Like any loyal canine, as Murph turned out to be, he chose to focus his attention on our companionship rather than the pain in his hindquarters.

In his vivid dreams, however, Murph saw all the world around him as pure adventure. In some of his dreams, the hound ran so fast that his feet left the earth, and he flew above this whole world he knew so well from ground-level. The farm was laid out far below his gliding figure, like a dog's trail map.

From his dreamed vantage-point atop the dam, Murph saw the whole world from both sides. That is, he saw the lake on one side and the creek far below the dam on the other side, water tumbling down from the culvert-pipe like Niagara Falls. Dream-critters scurried up and down and across the erosion-deterrent vines and groundcover. These plants helped secure the surface-soil of the dam and provided protective cover for voles, field mice, garden snakes, and the like from large-winged predators and clever four-legged canines, including fox, coyote, and hound. Murph saw the dam wall as one large living creature.

When the hound first showed up unexpectedly at my farm, it was a small miracle, for both of us. I'd been reminiscing of late the lanky Bluetick, Jackson, I'd had for Liz when she was little. Come to think of it, I guess maybe all my hounds over the years have come to me wounded in one way or another. Jackson had apparently been hit by a car as a pup. The result was a bad left hind hip and leg. He could stand on four legs, but only run on three. He was, all at once, humorous and tolerant guardian and sometimes pillow for my young daughter. The idea of getting another Bluetick had drifted in and out of my thoughts, of late.

I was in the wide hall of my sturdy, rebuilt pole-barn, moving hay square-bales off the flatbed-trailer into an empty stall for winter storage and ease of access. It was early autumn. The hardwoods along the creek had already started changing color, due to the unusually large number of cloudy days we were having then. The air was cool and crisp that evening, with a drizzle of cold raindrops falling outside.

As I sunk my grandfather's old hay-hook into the next bale, drawing back on it till the hook caught on the thick baling-wire, I felt something pressing against my leg. I looked down upon a sad, emaciated creature, too weary to raise even his own genetically sad hound-eyes up at me. The spotted dog was spent, on his last leg, leaning on mine just to hold himself up. His young, exhausted body shivered uncontrollably. His short hair coating was soaked. I took my barn-coat off the flatbed rail where I'd hung it, leaned down, and draped the pathetic hound. The denim coat seemed heavier than the dog as I lifted him up. His bony head flopped over my shoulder as I carried him toward the cab of the dually pickup. I laid the poor thing on the rear seat, and he was out. Fast asleep. I thought maybe dead.

Having unhooked the flatbed trailer, I climbed into the cab and grabbed my cellphone from the console. It was dark outside, but only about nine o'clock so I rang John, the local vet. I knew he would not be amused that I was interrupting him at home over my concerns for a stray, near-dead dog instead of a colt's bad cholic or a breeched calf. He agreed to meet me at the clinic by ten to see what he could do to help.

I drove out of the barn into the rain, across the barnyard, and down the road toward the closest pasture gate. Lightning struck nearby as I got out of the truck and approached the metal gate that hung on metal hinges attached to the old heavy-gauge iron pipe fencing that surrounded my farm. The hair stood up on the back of my neck. I didn't like being near metal fences or gates during lightning strikes. I hastily released the chain from between the two gate panels and secured one side against its receiving post.

I pulled up onto the county road, got out of the idling truck and reversed the gate procedure just performed. Lightening flashed in rapid succession on all sides in the dark. Immediate thunder-clap responses rattled the windows. As I raced toward the vet's clinic on the edge of town, I realized I was imagining that it was Jackson, my old dog, weak and asleep in the rear seat. Jackson was stolen from me long ago, and I never found him.

Almost sliding off the wet road, peering into an even heavier downpour, I slowed down, collected my thoughts, and focused on getting to the vet's in one piece. We got there. I pulled up to the back door of the clinic, barely visible through the deluge. I kneeled on the console of the big dually and rubbed the long hound's body through my barn coat, then put my hand on his chest to see if he was still breathing. He was, just. My own heart was pounding, and my head hurt. I settled back into the driver's seat, distracted by the dashboard display lights. I turned off the ignition and fell fast asleep, lulled by the consistent sound of the heavy rain falling onto the truck's hood and windshield.

I was rudely awakened by vet John's action of yanking my door open and shouting "Are you coming in or not? Can't you hear your phone?!" I'd slept right through the ringing, actually. Now the best horse and large animal vet in Barnes County was also soaked and shivering, all because of a sick, stray dog that I had brought to him in the middle of the night. He grumbled audibly as I followed him through the back door, trailing water like a cascade, frail hound in my arms.

~

My memory of Murph's unexpected arrival in the barn is as vivid as my recall of his departure. Murph was a gift of the universe for me, as I was for him. His scrappy stand-in, the self-named hound, Nike, was a loving gift from Clara and her dad. They delivered her to me, pulling up at the barn in their old pickup, during the last few days of the raw grief I felt over having lost Murph. Nike knew not of that history, of course, and sat erect on Clara's lap, wide-eyed and eager to get on with adventures at the farm. Clara has a natural affinity with four-legged critters, and I suspect that the teen may well wind up being a large-animal vet before too long.

One morning, with a blazing sunrise on the eastern horizon, I was in the office above the stables, going over inventory and new seed orders. I expected to see Murph soon, arriving for breakfast wet and disheveled from a long night of mournful howling at treed creatures. I heard Clara's old pickup rattling its noisy way slowly down the road to the barn. It was very early, on a school day. On a work-study schedule at the high school, Clara had classes in the morning and worked at the farm for me in the afternoons.

Glancing down from my second-floor studio, I noticed something was in the bed of her truck. Probably a bag of some new organic alfalfa cubes, or such, that her vegetarian friend Margaret wanted for Tofu, her pampered filly.

"Mr. Bartlett?" the teen called up from below. I went to the head of the stairs and said, "Good morning, Clara." I could see she was trying to hold back tears, but fresh ones streaked her cheeks. I descended the stairs. She took my hand in earnest and walked me to the bed of the truck. She gripped my arm with both hands, as if holding on for dear life.

There, on the floor, lay the dead body of Murphy, my beloved boon companion, my handsome Bluetick Coonhound. Clara had tenderly placed the hound on a big piece of cardboard, covering his body as best she could with her khaki barn coat. She sobbed in grief, not for herself, but knowing how horrific a shock this was for me. I put my arm around her, patting her on the shoulder, and said "It's OK, Clara, we'll survive this." I let the tailgate down, sliding his cardboard bed toward me.

Beneath Clara's barn coat was a fine fellow. "My poor boy, what have you done?"

Clara stood beside me, her hand reached out, gently holding a spotted hind foot. She spoke, between deep, sad breaths. "I saw him just up the road, just laying there in the grass on the shoulder."

Sobbing, she continued haltingly, "I knew something was wrong...I saw him on the way to school...oh, gosh, I'm so sorry...just laying there...all alone."

"He wasn't alone, Clara, once you found him. He was OK then. You did right by him."

"I just wanted to get him home."

"You're a good friend, Clara. To me, and to Murph. But you need to get on to school. You can help me bury him this afternoon, OK?"

"Oh, yes, please let me help you do that."

Clara helped me lower Murph from the tailgate down onto soft new rye grass.

Murphy, of course, never knew what hit him. Most evenings, just at deep sunset, I could coax him easily into the barn with bedtime words or a dog biscuit. But some nights, if I was delayed, or if he'd picked up an irresistibly tempting scent of a wild thing that needed chasing up a tree or down a hole in the ground, he would howl all night in the distance, rushing down through creek beds, bramble and briar, or in hot pursuit, he might foolishly dash across the county road just at the moment a ton-and-a-half with a big bumper hits his bony hip, the one full of pellets, and sends him spinning, dead already, onto the soft grass shoulder.

I'm certain his last thought and image was of the curly tailed rear-end of a smelly feral hog trying to outrun him. The pursued target ahead was the last thing he saw.

~

Often, in North Texas, winter arrives with no transition, no "heads up." No pleasant fall afternoons of cooling air and sunshine. No time to enjoy cutting firewood while a refreshing autumn breeze cools your brow. No, at these times, winter just blows in with a wet, cold fury.

We had about eight hours of rain on Monday at the farm. Forty-mile-an hour winds and temps in the forties, graphically pronounced all the winter prep chores yet undone. Sunday's near eighty temperature and clear sky was a quickly lost memory.

All in one day, everything changes at the farm when winter blows in. All thoughts of pleasant days leisurely watching the fall garden turn green with beds full of organic spinach, arugula, oak-leaf lettuce, chervil and the like, are replaced with sheer panic because emergency covers for the beds are unprepared. Fears of too much cold rain, too little sunshine. A friend, who lives in town, sees you at the Post Office and asks, "Why are you wearing a coat already?" "Come up to the farm" I answer. Even language becomes more efficient, less engaging, during winter's first attack. A sense of urgency arrives with each new cold blast. The change in weather manifests itself in the behavior of horses and livestock in graphic ways. The sheep are much happier with colder temps and don't spend so much time seeking shady spots. Cows no longer stand shoulder deep in the tank to ward off pesky flies. Their normally attendant exotic cowbirds are greatly diminished.

What do they eat in winter, I wonder? Do they migrate to tropical climes? The fish are eating less as the lake water grows colder, and they stay deeper in the warmer water below.

Chickens roost earlier and huddle together. My teen farmhands, unusually quiet, hurriedly round up heat lamps, extension cords and insulated waterer covers for the poultry palaces. The waterer covers look like extra-large British teapot cozies, but they do the job.

Horses get frisky with the arrival of winter. Heads and tails high in the air, they prance, spin and run for no other reason than the feel of new cold air rushing through those big nostrils. The grass is cool in their mouths. But the best treat about winter for the horses is the annual appearance of whole corn in their feed buckets. Horses love corn. They relish its crunch and distinctive flavor, and it adds warmth to their bellies.

The resident connoisseur of corn on our farm is none other than Solomon, the Wise (our mini donkey). We have temporarily moved cows and sheep to new pasture next door for a month or so. Old friend Bill came for an end-of-fall visit recently. He brought some prize herding dogs with him to round up everybody for two trips in his extra-long, gooseneck livestock trailer. The herding and trip to new pasture included Sol.

The neighbors' I'm leasing from will enjoy having Sol and Caesar, the big Pyrenees/Akbash, on the property for a month's visit. The new pasture is close enough for me to check on my small herd and flock daily. Corn has helped restore Sol's wounded ego.

The move to new pasture required Sol's separation from his pals, his fellow equines, Blaze and Samson. He did not take to it kindly. He is, after all, in his own mind, a fine-looking quarter horse too. Since he doesn't look in the mirror a lot, we figure he must also see himself just about their size. So we've started tossing a bit of corn into his feed now that cold weather is back.

As I mentioned before, Sol was originally hired to protect the sheep from marauding coyotes and bobcats. He was a very young employee, just a boy really. There was a period of adjustment, which he made just fine. He slowly began to watch out for his wards (in between bouts of tormenting them). He learned to occasionally look up from his grazing in the rye grass to locate where they were. When he felt it was needed, he would position himself along a virtual perimeter line and keep the sheep more or less clustered within that boundary. They learned to oblige and continue foraging without complaint.

But early on in his bodyguard employment, Solomon had the luxury of discarding his flock when the fancy struck him, blithely running off to play with Blaze and Samson. Sol can snort and kick and run and make loud noises with the best of them. In other words, as he would put it, to be a horse. Now the work has gotten serious. It's just Sol and serious, no non-sense Caesar, guarding the wooly flock, surrounded by tall grass and the sound of coyotes as the sun goes down.

As I expected, the little ass has proven himself worthy. He has matured and accepts his mission without question. However far and wide the sheep forage, Sol keeps an unobtrusive vigilant distance, slowly circling and watching throughout the day.

At dusk, the donkey shepherd moves his flock to the safety of their makeshift sheepfold near the neighbor's barn. He relishes his own corn ration while watching his charges enjoy their evening meal.

Each morning, the new pasture's temporary donkey-renter is greeted, over a graduated fence, by a couple of the neighbor's big draft Belgians. A friendly pair of giants, Mutt and Jeff, are nevertheless intrigued at the sight and presence of such a tiny equine creature in their midst.

∼

I'm looking out through a friend's picture-window, viewing an explosion of red leaves on the old pear tree in her front yard. It's a bright, cool day, and I'm enjoying watching yellow and golden leaves float down from a big pecan and a tall sycamore on the place. Annie's old friend, Bonnie, has a little 1940s bungalow near downtown Weatherford, and it's a kind of a getaway for us when we feel a need for some urban town time together. Bonnie travels the world as a food writer. She writes about the history of food in different cultures, and the occasional cookbook about regional dishes. It's convenient for our respective calendars, because Bonnie is on the road so much, we can pretty much come over on a whim or when the fancy strikes us. It's a symbiotic relationship. We can stay here pretty much whenever we need an urban fix. And Bonnie has the pick of our garden, whatever she wants to experiment with for her latest book project. We plant things just for her and Annie to try out in our kitchen when need be.

This morning we were up early, enjoying our coffee on the front porch. We cheered the runners (and walkers) streaming by us on their way to the Square during the last leg of their annual run through the Historic District as one of the opening ceremonies for the city's Holiday Festival downtown. The city Christmas Tree was lit last night midst red-cheeked crowds of revelers and diners strolling through the many colorful stalls and tents of vendors and artisans. Downtown merchants were open late, serving shoppers who juggled arms full of bags stuffed with toys, kitchen gadgets, apparel, perfumes, linens, plus weekend supplies of libations, and organic groceries, all available on the Square.

This time of year, our fall and winter garden at the farm is bountiful with greens and herbs. Annie and I come up with recipes to share with customers at the Farmers Market, and we grow many items specifically for the needs of individual chefs. The current recipes we're working on benefit from fresh, organic items like Greek oregano, Hill Hardy rosemary, chocolate mint, French Rocket arugula, Mexican Mint Marigold (with edible yellow flowers), Genovese basil, French tarragon, cilantro, English thyme, Italian parsley and garlic chive (my favorite, and is much more complementary for baked potatoes than the ubiquitous onion chive).

Edible flowers are a big hit with the chefs, and we try to keep them supplied throughout the year. Spring is a bounty of opaque nasturtiums in every color. They look like I just painted them with enamel. They only last a couple of weeks, three at the most, but a couple of our chef customers plan dishes annually around their colorful arrival.

Probably my favorite is pineapple sage, with long, fuchsia-shaped flowers that are sweet, and taste divinely like the first time you ate a honeysuckle blossom as a kid. The leaves add a distinctive pineapple flavor and scent to the richness of the sage. Along with our striped Russian Red garlic cloves pressed into slits in pork roast, one chef always inserts several leaves of the pineapple sage curled into tight bundles. Annie makes a lovely aromatic tea with the pineapple sage leaves, something she enjoyed as a child with her grandmother. Though the sage grows all summer into fall, the flowers stop blooming for the duration of the hottest months, but right on schedule, the bright red, sweet beauties return every fall. Sage goes dormant in the winter, the trunks becoming woody and barren of foliage. But it's one of the most dependably perennial plants in the garden. Our current crop is several years old.

The serrano and cayenne pepper plants are robust and productive, plus a few sweet peppers and marble-sized Loco peppers. The tiny round loco peppers are very hot but release a lot of vibrant unique flavor. I don't grow ghost peppers because I find them just painfully hot, but without interesting flavor.

For our own kitchen, we still get one or two lemon cucumbers every day, and the Nantes carrots and Detroit Red Beets are perfect right now. The beautiful black zucchini won't make much more, but the soon-to-be-harvested winter Brussels sprouts and broccoli will make up for the loss. Our ground cherries (also called cherry-husk tomatoes) are about to give up what with the cold nights, but still gift us with a few of the sweet little vellum-wrapped gems.

We have a bumper crop of white, sweet onions. We will plant garlic and shallots in late December. In years past, I've always planted these in late January, but after all we *are* a Zone 8 now (thanks to climate change). I may plant bananas next year!

We continue enjoying big plates of salad greens (fresh and wilted): Chinese cabbage, collard and mustard greens, rainbow chard, and Tatsoi, a Korean heirloom mustard with small, perfectly round dark green leaves that taste like sweet spinach. The Tatsoi has become popular with our chef clients.

Night temperatures have been kind to the garden, though on three separate occasions in recent weeks we had to bring out the freeze-cloth and cover everything. We don't normally worry about it unless the temp drops several degrees under thirty. Poor basil, of course, pretty much gives up the ghost with sustained nights of forty degrees, covered or uncovered.

With winter upon us, I crave pasta, soups, and stews, braised and poached items and Chinese stir frys, so down come the stockpots, woks, and steam-baskets from their elevated summer perches high atop kitchen cabinets. For a cold-weather treat the other night, we served Bonnie a dinner of Annie's incredibly delicious braised, locally farmed, veal shanks. The meat had been marinated for three days and melted like butter in the mouth. Annie prepared the dish as a kind of riff on *osso buco*, a favorite of mine, first experienced long ago during a semester I taught in Italy.

~

It was late for any chickens to be out, and I had been looking for Dee for some time. "Dee" was short for Dorothy, named after a bossy aunt of mine. Lately the hen had taken to making nests for herself in various piles of hay, including the hay in livestock feeders. I'm sure the occasional horse or ewe really enjoys coming upon a tasty organic egg to go along with their hay portion, but that service is not really in Dee's job description. In the background, I could hear the tractors' cold engines puttering, trying to idle properly, as I always cranked them over to run for a short while on such frigid nights.

All the other hens were in the coop roosting for the night, but Dee was not to be found. Two ram lambs, being fattened for market, were housed in an unused horse stall in the barn. They were the last on that night's feeding list. Just as I opened the stall door, I heard Dee squawking hen-talk reprimands at me as she fretfully performed her version of the Texas Two-Step beneath the jostling lambs. The sounds of the running tractors must have muffled her appeals for help when I was outside the barn. So there I was, trying to figure out how to reach down to pick her up, while avoiding spilling the rams' feed bucket or releasing my grip on the door so as not to let the lambs loose. Dee saw the solution and squawked at my ineptness. The lambs were focused on the feed bucket, not on her, but they were stomping all around her as they adjusted this way and that for a better head-thrust-into-the-bucket position.

Wisely, Dee decided to hop up onto the back of the lamb nearest me. He gave her no notice, his nose adroitly following the swinging bucket like radar. She stood there on his back, gripping the shifting wool, and looked at me as if to say, "OK, I've done my part. The rest is up to you, fella."

She gave me just the few seconds I needed to turn, latch the door, and shift the bucket to my right hand. When I turned around, Dee was still riding wool and I simply scooped her up with my left hand. As my sidekick, Annie, had trained her to do, the flustered Rhode Island Red hen finally laid her pretty head on my chest and relaxed, safe and warm in the fold of my arm. With the free hand, I poured dinner out for the fat, hungry lambs.

It's a wonderful feeling to get the last of the critters settled and fed for the night. To have the orange colt, Blaze, secured away in a stall with his short pal, Sol, the miniature donkey. To have the female lambs and ewes closed into the sheepfold for the night. To have blankets firmly attached on Samson and all the horse herd. Even the barn kittens wound down their play, and moved closer to the barn where they pass the cold nights, snuggled into their favorite warm nooks.

Collecting the dogs Spin and Nike, we walked back up the hill to the barn beneath a clear, dark winter sky of stars. Winter is the best time to see the night heavens. Spin's cattle-dog head was erect, scanning the night horizon for intruders, and Nike's noble hound-dog nose pressed on the cold ground, drawing in scents like a canine vacuum cleaner. In the distance, we could hear cold and hungry coyotes, tracing the perimeter of the neighboring farms. Nike, the loud hound, paused and looked in the direction of the haunting yells and barks. Old Spin spun in circles around us, eager to tuck into her cozy dog-bed in the barn's wide hallway. Her priorities were clear. The younger Nike held her hound instincts in check, but only because I was beside her.

Coyotes are a handsome lot. Beautifully sleek and wily creatures, yet unwanted by civilization, to be sure. They howl and mourn at a distance. They are the banished. No one prepares a meal and a warm place to sleep for their kind, even though "coyote art" abounds in yards and on mantles in sheet metal and painted silhouettes of their tragic forms. They are beneath contempt from farmers and home-owners who work hard to secure timid, domestic critters from the fiendish attacks of coyotes and wolves. But you must admire their stealth and survival skills. In dark fields at the edges of concrete alleys and fenced back-yards of even the best-lit, priciest new housing developments, coyotes wait and watch.

Gubbio, Italy, is home to famous poems, songs and artworks dedicated to one historic canine. As the legend goes, this particular wolf was no longer satisfied with hanging back at the edges of the pretty hill-top village, sneaking in at night to raid the errant pie left on a windowsill and the like. No, this wolf got bold. He began to attack whenever he liked, not just stealing food and biting pets and people, but eating babies and chasing townsfolk in the middle of the day.

Enter St. Francis, who loved animals and preached to them. The master proto-Renaissance artist, Giotto, illustrated such touching scenes in murals and altarpiece panels. Frescos lining the nave walls in Assisi's San Francesco Basilica narrate the life of the saint. Included is a depiction of St. Francis gently sermonizing to a flock of small birds gathered on the ground, all attentively listening, save one. The errant fellow has been a reluctant listener on an upper tree branch, who decides to drop down and join the congregation so he can hear the kind saint's advice better.

Apparently, St. Francis had heard of the dreaded "Wolf of Gubbio," as the terrible creature had come to be called. Francis went to the town. The townsfolk feared the wolf would harm or kill the famous monk, but of course the wretched wolf was no match for one of St. Francis's sermons. The wolf repented of his evil ways, stopped killing, and Francis mediated a compromise whereby the townsfolk adopted the wolf and provided it sustenance. To this day, the converted Wolf of Gubbio is celebrated on the town's famous pottery, tiles, and paintings. The wolf became the proud emblem of the town.

~

Today's cloudless mid-December morning was a visual feast. The whole northern sky was a rich Cobalt blue; one pure sheet of color that spanned the entire horizon. The horses and Solomon, having finished their early breakfast oat rations, were turned out into the front pasture. Tails high in crisp thirty-eight-degree air, they frolicked like children in a playground of lush green winter rye grass.

The dog gang, Caesar, Nike, Blackie, Spin, and Tommy Cat joined me for an early morning reconnoiter of the farm and environs. Sometimes the animals ebbed and flowed in slow circles around my legs like water in a stream. One or two would catch the scent of some hidden wild critter not far off the trail but didn't stray for long away from the farm's canine pack.

We descended into the old bois d'arc grove, now replete with golden yellow leaves.

Our shared journey across the narrow, shaded draw took us beneath a canopy of translucent gold foliage on blue sky. The scene reminded me of the glittering interior surfaces of the thirteenth century Sainte Chapelle in Paris, which features the tallest of Gothic stained-glass lance-shaped windows. As clouds move along the Seine, just outside, playing with the sun's rays, the chapel interior becomes like a rock concert's psychedelic light show.

Now and then, a small cascade of leaves would slowly flicker down upon us like gold foil ornament. The canine gang paused with me as I stood for a moment, letting my senses take in the cold, the quiet, and the color. We enjoyed each other's company, as centuries of dogs and humans had done before us, a symbiosis of species.

Starting our ascent up the other side of the draw, my companions enjoyed a strenuous race up the steep incline. They waited for me at the cusp of the ridge, silhouetted like ancient sentry sculptures against the bright blue sky. Upon my ascent, I was greeted with a chorus of enthusiastically wagging tails and smiling faces.

I've not always seen the sky so vividly blue. For years, the sky had turned a tarnished pale blue to my eyes. Most of us don't notice the gradual color change that develops with cataracts. We hold onto a childhood memory of the color blue, our older mind's eye dulling us into a kind of tolerance for lesser blues and greens. Everybody gets cataracts eventually, but they creep up on you.

Claude Monet fought his cataracts with medications and custom-prescribed glasses, and finally agreed to surgery in 1923. Subsequently, Monet destroyed dozens of his own paintings because he saw that they were not done in the colors he intended. He then proceeded to finish the last of his brilliantly blue Water Lily paintings. His friend Mary Cassatt, America's own Impressionist painter, ended her career because of cataracts. Her cataract surgery was a failure. Cassatt died blind in 1926.

Like most folks, my cataract surgeries were several years apart. My right eye's cataract "ripened" so quickly that a cloud formed over most of my field of vision in that eye. I was having coffee on the porch when it happened. Startled, I went into the kitchen to tell Annie. She looked up from the table and immediately said "Sam! Something's wrong in your eye." She looked closely and declared, "Wow. It's a cataract. White like a cloud." Then she hugged me, patting my back as if I was a child. In the mirror's reflection, it looked the size of a small white navy bean.

The day the bandage was removed from my right eye, the surgeon's smile was enhanced with a beautifully intense blue-violet tie. Annie was seated behind him, grinning hopefully up at me.

She wore a starched white shirt with pockets and a big collar. The shirt was such a pure reflective white, it was painful to see. The doctor had promised me that my right eye would see the world's colors as I did as a youngster. He did not lie. I gave him a big hug.

A couple of years ago, the remaining cataract from my left eye was removed, so that I no longer see muddied warm colors on the left, and true cool colors on the right. Stereo vision works for me now in both eyes, not just for shapes and perspective, but also in living color.

I'm reminded of when I first started painting in earnest, as a young airman/printer. North Dakota's vast, uninterrupted sky was blinding in saturated blueness. White houses looked blue in shadow. The tarmac of flight runways reflected a dark, sea-blue from beneath transparent, gray layers, like rich Rembrandt-school glazes. In winter, on sunny days, any moisture in the air froze into myriad ice-crystal prisms that reflected tiny kaleidoscopic colors all around you.

At the farm, the dogs and I followed a path that paralleled the cow pasture, where four red rectangular Devon heifers grazed peacefully. We strolled past the small orchard of hundred-year-old hard-shell pecan trees, alive with young squirrels chasing each other like fluid streams of fur. Round and round the grand trunks they raced like ribbons, if not leaping tree to tree from sturdy branches. The dog gang paid the squirrels no mind, their tongues lolling about in mid-air, thirsty from our long hike.

Sensing the barn in the near distance, they all sprinted toward familiar water bowls they could see in their minds' eye, waiting to replenish them in the wide hall between horse stalls. Even old Spin, who sees only indistinct light and dark shapes these days, sped glee-fully, following the pack with abandon, and with her nose and ears. I prayed she wouldn't run headlong into the closed barn doors, due to the large visible cataracts clouding her vision.

Elysia is decked out in its finest holiday attire. Downtown looks like a Lionel Train Christmas village. One afternoon, coming out of the Post Office, I watched a group of scouts helping with the decoration of the bandstand and the city Christmas tree. Each year, a humble cedar tree is transformed into a grand, sparkling vision that delights the eye. Shop windows downtown are festooned with garland, decorations, and colorful lights for the season. The Ronning's Family Bakery always has an amazing display which spans the entire storefront. Glistening cakes and pies and pastries are framed in windows draped in colorful lights and ancient decorations. Strolling past the magical scene in late evening, the yeasty aromas alone seduce passersby to stop in for a jam-filled *Krapfen*. Everybody's a kid again with one of those treasures in hand.

Coming home the other evening through town, Nike and I both did double takes as we witnessed an unusual, splendid sight on Main. Nike, the young Bluetick Coonhound, always rides shotgun in the pickup, as did her predecessor hound, Murph. She sits up straight, proud of her handsome foal's coat this time of year. The Methodist Church's "living nativity" tableau this season included a huge, live, camel, complete with all the finest riding regalia befitting a Wise Man's mount. The big fellow was very popular, surrounded by happy children and parents as it munched hay and blinked giant eyes back at its admirers. The three very small Wise Men and assorted short shepherds were wary, but game, children trying their best to remain in place, despite their close proximity to the giant camelid's tall legs. Nike's long muzzle hung open in amazement at such an apparition. As we passed, she turned her elegant head to face me, as if to ask, "Did you see *that*?" I nodded to her in the affirmative. You just never know what you're going to see in downtown Elysia these days.

Our living holiday tableau at the farm includes many pleasant winter images. Recently, on every rail of the two metal gates that open onto the road down to the barn, dozens of bright red cardinals were busily chirping to each other. Our rusty metal gates had become a resting place for the various cardinal families to roost and enjoy a holiday visit.

Two new additions to the farm's menagerie are very photogenic Devonshire heifers. Devons are a heritage breed of cattle, and appear, in profile, to be perfect horizontal rectangles. The Dutch modernist painter, Mondrian, would have loved these pure red, right-angled rectangular heifers. One of the earliest livestock breeds brought to American shores from England, the Devon's milk has the highest butterfat content of all cows. It's what "Devonshire cream" products are made from. The modern Devon has been bred for superior beef as well as dairy markets.

For now, all the high school farm hands have had fun helping to wean the little red heifers. Timid at first, the girls now eat out of hand or bucket at close enough range for petting their curly forelocks, which they seem to never tire of.

Formal introductions of the other farm occupants occur every day. Yesterday, I noticed the guinea hens had decided to pay a visit to the youngsters. The closer the hens got to say a proper hello, the more skittish the heifers became, and in turn, the louder the guineas became. If you've been around them, you know how deafening their hen-chatter can become. In addition, the sudden furtive flights of these odd fowl can startle the biggest of God's creatures. That's why they make such good watchdogs. Trust me, Devon heifers and guinea hens together make for quite a rodeo.

There's nothing like new animal babies to invigorate the farm. Solomon and Blaze, the orange colt, are constantly peering over the fence (well, under the fence, in Sol's case) to get a look at the little Devon sisters. The older Tunis ewes stand at the gate separating the calf pen from the sheepfold to admire the handsome red heifers. The younger barn cats have selected the calf pen as their current wrestling arena, to keep a closer eye on the new tenants. The energy and enthusiasm of these young creatures encourage a sense of well-being and hope for the New Year. It will certainly be entertaining, and we don't have to drive anywhere to enjoy it.

Trees at the farm these winter days look like penciled line drawings on gray paper. A mile away, you can see a neighbor's house through the leafless limbs of trees that, for most of the year, completely obscure the structure. Livestock and pens that normally go unnoticed, absorbed into verdant foliate landscapes, become visible and easily recognizable to roadside passersby as winter advances. Wild residents, like our local fox den, go deeper into the woods for better cover, and are more quickly spotted at the exposed edges of their hunting grounds.

I recall one cold, dark night at Granny's house (my maternal grandmother) when I was a boy. It was a hard winter in Irene. There was lots of snow and sleet that year. There were also lots of wolves that winter—hungry wolves. On that late night, a semi-circle of men stood in Granny's parlor. The men included my uncles Buck, Wink, and Audie, my dad, Will, and a few other friends from town and neighboring farms.

They stood awkwardly, yet respectfully, in the presence of Granny and her doily-covered parlor furniture. Men and boys alike in my family knew not to sit on the parlor furniture, except on rare occasions like Christmas Day, or after a relative's funeral. The men shifted their weight from one leg to the other, uncomfortably shuffling their boots forward and back in a kind of contrapposto pose. They were kind of like stiff marble sculptures, trying to stay in one place without breaking anything.

Each man said, "Thank you, ma'am" (even her own sons), as Granny and my mother served them hot coffee in translucent bone china cups and a palm-sized fried apricot pie apiece. The normally confident men reverted to clumsy boys, as the delicate cups clinked like crystal in their weathered hands. Balancing saucer and cup and Granny's famous fried apricot pie was too demanding a trial for any man.

I stayed on the big room's perimeter, standing in the dining room doorway, or the entry vestibule portal, or this or that corner, watching quietly. This was about men's business, and kids needed to be invisible. Each man juggled his bone china coffee cup, a hot pie, and a gun. The assorted arsenal of hunting weapons around the room included small and large rifles and shotguns. One neighbor wore an old family pistol, holstered at his hip. I recognized a .22 and a .410 that I had hunted with. I was too small for the others. The men were bundled up for serious business outside and were anxious to leave the heat of the big pot-bellied stove. The men were going out into the cold, silent night to hunt livestock-marauding wolves.

This was the same group of men who stood in Granny's parlor on a later occasion, another cold winter's night. Snow stood tall outside that night too, but there was good humor in the room.

On this particular night, the circle of friends and family juggled the same bone china coffee cups saucers, more fried pies, shovels instead of firearms by their sides. Granny seemed happy, and I couldn't believe my eyes at the sight of wide barn scoops and shovels in the parlor! I stood in the room with the men on this occasion, enjoying a fried pie myself, and good-natured teasing from my uncles. The men laughed loudly. Granny was amused at them and kept shaking her head, in a fun way, at their boyish enthusiasm.

Uncle Buck was there, our family's genuine bronc- and bull-riding rodeo star. Buck served in the navy, in the Pacific, for three years, right up to the end of World War II. When Granny tearfully greeted his return home at the Hubbard train station, he had just turned nineteen. Uncle Wink, who could repair any machine just with a piece of baling wire, had driven a tank for Patton in the same war. Uncle Audie was the oldest and had pretty much stopped talking after surviving the war. He loved his family but just didn't have much to say. Audie spent his days on the tractor, peacefully plowing, plowing, plowing the land in a kind of thanksgiving ritual.

The Hanson brothers were there, too, juggling their china cups. Dub and Howard were distant relatives and running mates of Uncle Buck. They were famous rodeo legends in their own right. Dub trained the best cutting horses, and Howard the roping stock. All three were high school chums who spent their late teens fighting a war overseas, far from Texas sunsets and stars.

They made a pact that if they got home alive, they'd make up lost time and have some fun, far away from farming. Rodeo was their recovery, applause and appreciative whistles from the crowd their reward.

At one end of Granny's parlor, the pot-bellied stove cheerily warmed the room. At the other end, the room was warmed by the presence of a huge Christmas tree, gaily festooned with countless family decorations, generations old. The joyous gathering was prelude to the men going sledding, in their fashion. I was sure that my dad and Uncle Buck had been tipping a few drinks outside the house and must have mischievously talked the others into bringing the shovels indoors with them, hoping to get a rise out of Granny. Her joy of having these men gathered in the parlor again, boys who she watched grow up and some that she bore herself, overrode concerns that her hand tatted lace doilies might get stained. I'd never seen her that relaxed, that happy.

A steep ravine of a long-since-dried-out creek bed bordered the edge of Granny's front pasture. Each reveler had brought a wide barn shovel, snow shovel, or scoop on which to descend the slope. They would soon plop down on the shovels, ostensibly steering with the handles before them and speed down the snow-covered ravine. Injuries were likely.

During this holiday season, I fondly remember the men of my family on those two frigid nights. On the one night, they were, of necessity, deadly serious, with a communal mission to protect live-stock. On the other, they were just a group of big boys having a party in front of glittering holiday lights, anxious to get outside and play in the snow.

Blaze, the orange colt

THREE

Tomatoes and Tornadoes

A new "weekend farmer" couple recently bought twelve acres of the old Wilson homestead, about a half a mile south of my place. Eager to celebrate their move to the country, I guess, they decided to start the new year with a big bang. They put on an impressive New Year's Eve fireworks show but failed to alert their farming neighbors of the big, loud event. Maybe they just forgot to warn us, but that sure would have saved a lot of grief for folks hereabouts.

The unexpected pyrotechnics were very professional. It would rival any North Texas municipality's official public display. The night sky over our place was alight with streaking colors and sparkling confetti-lights from exploding fountains and rockets for hours. It lit up the historic cemetery between our place and theirs like some creepy horror movie. At times, our arena pen and barn buildings would suddenly be completely illuminated in eerie floodlight, like the flare scenes in Coppola's *Apocalypse Now*.

Near-sonic booms followed, which rattled tin-siding and roofs. Colorful heritage breed chickens scattered everywhere, blasted off their roosts, and stopped laying for days.

The horses were eating from a round bale in the arena when the first flare-and-bomb effect hit. They raced to the far corners of the east pasture to get as far away as possible. To this day, the youngsters Sol and Blaze only come back to the barn long enough to empty their buckets of alfalfa cubes, oats, and corn. They don't go into the arena pen at night anymore, choosing to enjoy the hay bale only under daylight.

Spin, the heeler, and Murph, the hound, were all over the back screen-door like frantic banshees. They were shaken from their cozy sleeping spots in the barn's wide hallway by the first explosions. I let them onto the back porch where they huddled like frightened children. I peered out toward the bois d'arc grove between the house and the barn, which seemed strangely alive in the weird, moving lights of the fireworks.

I, myself, was in the den nodding off in my favorite easy chair when the frantic dogs hit the back door, rousting me. Annie, asleep on the couch, turned and covered her head with the colorful quilt her grandmother made for her long ago. Some years past, we'd decided that New Year's Eve on the road is for amateurs. You know, "Been there. Done that."

It was when I went out on the back porch to settle Murph and Spin down I noticed that Caesar, the one-year-old Pyrenees, wasn't with the others. I let the dogs come inside to escape the war zone. They followed me to the front door, where I expected to find Caesar sleeping on the welcome mat. No big white pup. I remembered then that the last time I had seen the boy was down at the barn, shortly before the first firecracker went off.

He and Spin were in my way in a stall I was cleaning out, so I'd run them off, then taken a last look at the roosting chickens, and headed up the hill to the house. Hound and heeler had returned to the barn behind me, and out of habit, I must have assumed Caesar followed them as usual, after carefully re-marking his territory in the dark.

I searched for Caesar, the pup, till three in the morning, New Year's Day. I phoned all the neighbors' places throughout the night, leaving voicemails for those who didn't answer. Yes, they had seen and heard the big fireworks show. Yes, their animals fled for cover too.

They'd keep their eyes out for the big, friendly fellow. Nobody minded me waking them about a lost dog.

I was up at six, printing posters. We posted Caesar's face and phone number wherever we thought people might be likely to see him. We attached his picture to surrounding entrance gates and rural mailboxes. We had no idea in which direction he had lit out.

We left a poster at the police station in Elysia. The chief herself came to the door, expressed sympathy that we find Caesar soon, and kindly offered to place his photo where officers would see it going in and out. Apparently, we weren't the only ones looking for critters running from the explosions.

We pinned posters on the grocery store's popular bulletin board, the feed store, the Post Office, the front door of the local filling station; you name a place, we announced our loss with a picture of the missing pup. Slowly driving the white dually all day, in all directions, we loudly called out "Caesar!" into fields and pastures, over and over. The truck is his favorite ride. For that matter, the truck is probably his favorite napping spot, as it has a back-seat big enough for his large frame, with AC in the summer and heat in the winter.

Other Pyrenees chased us, dutifully running toward the road to let us know they were on guard with their deep-throated woof-threats. They followed us along their own fence lines, escorting us gruffly away from their domains, protective, as they are trained to be. Each time we were happy to see one of the big white dogs, and each time saddened that it wasn't ours.

My cell phone rang. A neighbor announced that Caesar had just crossed a nearby farm-to-market road in front of their pickup and was headed off between two fields. I had been headed in the opposite direction of the pup a couple of miles away, but now knew about where he was. He was a mess when we caught up with him, covered in grass and burrs and dirt, but what a grand sight he was, too. The joyful reunion was mutual. He was one exhausted fellow. He leapt onto the back seat, jostling his canine pals to the edges and floor. He fell fast asleep, relieved that he was home once more.

~

J anuary up at the farm has been like an unwanted ride on a merry-go-round that never returns to the same place. One day, I'm turning all the upstairs faucets on a slow-drip and setting space-heaters to the appropriate level for anticipated teens and twenties' temperatures. And the very next day I'm adjusting all for seventy-degree days and forty-degree nights! Thankfully, Clara and Margaret, who board Pickle and Tofu here, are thoughtful enough to take care of most of the frequent removal and reattachment of horse blankets as needed.

Yesterday, up on the crest of the hill, at the turn-around, I was appalled to find lots of damage rendered by the hooves of trespassing horses. They must have gotten through one of the gates separating the horse pasture up front from the herbs and produce. Since early morning, they had stayed all day, judging by the manure piles everywhere around the enclosed gardens. The outlaws got into the greenhouse and tore out one wall, taking with them two potting tables and all the containers of young seedlings.

Then the horses found the closed tubs of chicken feed, scratch, crushed oyster shells, and such in the open dog-run between the two chicken palaces. Tubs were upended and grain spread everywhere. What a wreck. What a waste. When not cursing, I wept.

While examining the damage to the greenhouse, I glanced over at one corner of the south-side chicken yard, only to spy several hens standing over a lone, reclining hen, pecking at her as she lay still in a hole. Not a good sign.

Sure enough, the hen in the hole was dead, and headless. Raccoon, probably. I stood in the chicken yard, looking around to try and figure out what had happened. Several other hens were missing tail-feathers, and of course, the count of hens was lacking. All country predators get hungry for caged targets in winter, sort of like how deer are hunted these days. I cleaned up the mess, distracting the pecking mourners with fresh grain. Then I traced the hot wire for the full length of both chicken yards, looking for possible "shorts" in the continuous wire stretched horizontally above the ubiquitous chicken-wire fence. I dread to think of how much I have spent over the past four years on hot wire chargers, transformers, batteries, wire, connectors, gate-joiners, and separators, just to protect my costly heritage-breed chickens and their marketable colorful eggs.

Of course fencing hens with hot wire is a drop in the bucket compared with hot wire and horses. You better have buckets of something other than equine love to fund that hobby.

I found the source of the short in the chicken yard hot wire. The industrial-sized solar panel on the southwest side of the building soaks up most of the sun's rays throughout the year, and it's mounted on a flexible arm so I can aim it accurately, more or less.

The insulated wire coming right out of the charger had slipped down behind the doorframe of the hen palace. It was obviously shorting out on a nail somewhere on the back of the door frame.

Additionally, the raccoon had adeptly climbed over the inoperative hot wire near the palace door. Two overlapping wires were pressed on top of each other, due to the heft of this masked marauder. The fat little critter probably got across the overlapping wires without a shock. I was insulted.

An hour or so after my discovery of the hot wire malfunction, I'd repaired everything by ensuring that all the wire was above or away from any obstruction or interference, and I checked that all the surviving poultry had plenty of food and water.

The charger acknowledged my hot wire efforts by throwing its little arm vigorously into the bright green range of the status-screen, the box pulsing with a steady rhythmic click, reassuring me that all was well with the world, hot wire wise.

Repairs done, my mind turns to the spring gardens. In the next week or so, I'll be planting February's seeds for Nantes carrots which will be thick and sliceable in sixty-five days, but I can never resist pulling the sweet orange treasures while babies, around forty days. Plant Napa-type cabbage seeds soon. They'll take about fifty days but won't bolt on you as quickly as others.

My experience with beets at the farm has been greatly rewarding (remember, I'm growing everything in raised beds or untilled, elevated gardens on organic soil and compost). Striped Chioggia and golden beets are beautiful on the table, but you can't beat the flavor of Bull's Blood, for the fat root itself, or for the delicious greens. Bulls Blood beets will get big in about sixty days up at our farm, and the green leaves can be harvested for salads in about forty days.

I plant lettuce and spinach seeds in early February, and any variety seems happy with that schedule. North Texas gardens produce spectacular greens these days, with prolific early winter and early spring crops. About the time the twenty-degree days of January subside, the soft earth of the raised beds is ready to accept new seeds for spring bounty. What sheer, childlike joy I get out of seeing the first green sprouts raise their little heads out of rich, dark soil. These days, I do start some garden plants in the greenhouse, but I still prefer to plant the seeds directly into Barnes County terroir, the base of all my raised beds.

Neither of my grandmothers had a greenhouse for the family vegetable gardens. They required only sturdy, tight garden fencing to keep the rabbits out, and a large collection of empty tin cans in various sizes for use as customized insulators for young sprouts. My method is partly empirical observation and partly nostalgic faith in the apocryphal soil education passed on to me by grandparents.

Daily observation of the progress of my gardens' plants convinces me that the seeds produce stronger, more resilient trunks if they can avoid the trauma of transplanting. My Swiss chard, kale, greens, radishes, and spinach will be popping up soon into the light, and they will be happy that their toes stay firmly gripping plenty of deep terroir. Soon, I'll get those seed potatoes into soft, living soil, with plenty of organic compost, leaves, and straw piled up on the mound.

As a boy, I helped Grandad Bartlett plant seed potatoes every year. From my earliest days in the garden with him, he would try to explain the phases of the moon to me. He would show me pictures and calendar dates in the *Old Farmer's Almanac*. Regardless of the moon's phase, it always seemed to me that we were planting seed potatoes on Valentine's Day. Grandad was a consistently good teacher. He let me use his sharp pocketknife to cut the seed potatoes correctly so that each piece had the maximum number of eyes possible.

I like to think that Grandad would enjoy helping me plant fingerlings, Yukon Gold, Kennebec, and Peruvian purples. Then again, he would probably regard so many choices as a bit fussy.

My old friend Bill Goodman raises dwarf Nigerian goats near Graham. The tiny white acrobats are honestly about the size of the little stuffed critters in a niece's massive collection of *My Little Pony* toys from her childhood. If you've taken your children to a petting zoo in the Dallas-Fort Worth area, you've likely seen offspring from Bill's miniature goat herd. It's always fun to visit Bill, talk plants, and sip iced tea on his back porch while watching the antics of the nearby indefatigable little Capra kids. Neighboring farmers would bring their own kids, ostensibly to just enjoy the barnyard circus, and often leave with a couple of the cute goats—and less cash in their wallets.

Bill is also a good gardener. We have traded tips, seeds, and labor over the years on many mutually beneficial farm projects. Like me, he planted and tended crops and gardens with his North Texas family from childhood through high school. Like me, he retired from a fulfilling career of many years (a radio-microwave engineer in his case) and went back to life in the country and to farming. His having accomplished a successful retirement transition, a couple of decades ahead of me, I've learned a lot from Bill.

Unlike me, Bill never rushes the transplanting of his young, vulnerable tomato plants. A bad habit I started, back when my adult brain turned my thoughts toward selling herbs and vegetables, was that I would set out my delicate tomato and basil plants too early. My purpose was not without merit, as my intention was to be first to show up at various farmers markets with ripe, delicious produce before anybody else, not to mention delivering to restaurant chefs truly local organic items early in the season.

Bill followed a spring planting schedule like my Granny's. Her motto: "Beware a late frost."

When asked, Bill always advises rookie farmers and gardeners not to set out tiny tomato plants before April 12, *period.* "Anywhere in North Texas, just don't plant tomatoes too early" he would counsel. I hate to be the one to say it, and it breaks my heart, but I must at least suggest that this crazy spring weather of late may be the undoing of Bill's longtime reliable method. At least, current conditions require constant monitoring, with ample frost cloth at the ready. The high temperature in our Barnes County gardens the other day was eighty-five degrees. The next night's low for us was thirty degrees.

Being cautious like Bill, I didn't jump the gun this year, and I waited to transplant all my tiny tomatoes until April 15. No sweat, I thought. I'll just sit back, and watch 'em grow, right? *NOT.*

So, the teen farmhands and I will yet again be dragging out the frost-cloth covers to protect the new tomato and basil plants for tonight's low thirties' temps. The tomatoes will probably be OK, but all the gorgeous little Genovese and Thai Sweet Basil plants will be in for a very rough night, even under the best frost cover. Basil basically doesn't like any temperature under forty-five degrees, covered or not.

As my farming family has always done, we hope and pray for good soil, sun, and rain. Should I plant too early, and nature sends a freeze, it's my own fault that plants will suffer.

This spring, my tiny heirloom tomato starters include Nyagous (a dark Russian heirloom), Black Prince (amazing flavor, and a favorite of our customers), and my preference, Cherokee Purple.

With some of the tomato transplants, my college daughter Liz, wanted to try a new procedure this year. She's planted some of the starters so that almost all the leaves on the trunk are covered with compost and straw. She's read that this method will supposedly encourage the covered lower branches to become new roots, strengthen the central trunk, and produce bigger yield.

For me, I've always been mindful over the years, regarding tomato plants, to follow the instructions of my Grannyt. I was taught to strip off the lowest two branches of leaves to increase girth of the lower trunk. Granted, that exercise was rather more easily achieved with small boyhood fingers than with arthritic ones. But I'm no slave to tradition. So I am curious to see what impact on productivity and plant strength my daughter's new experiment may have.

My Granny grew awesome tomatoes, always in terroir, though she would never have used that term. Granny had no green house. All seeds went directly into the garden's soil. As the first sprouts of the young tomato plants raised their little green heads, a protecting barrier (old coffee cans with both ends removed) would be installed around the tender trunk. providing cylindrical security against cold or strong northern spring gusts. In addition, the tin citadel would heat during sunlight hours, encouraging the impressionable youngster to grow up.

Granny's garden was watered by hand, from the well. At some point, one of her sons built a cozy well house, installed a pump and added a hydrant and hose for her. As I recall, she liked the pump but still trusted her old watering can more than the hose. She was still using it when I returned to Texas after four years in the Air Force. Granny was old school.

I won't go into detail about how she carefully instructed me and my cousins, when we were four and five years old, to help fertilize the garden. But we all clearly understood our responsibility to help save water. Every spring, she would point out exactly which plants were to be enhanced, whenever we needed to relieve ourselves. But God help the male child who was caught watering the wrong plant, in my Granny's eyes. New gardeners will find it interesting to peruse the list of contents on the package or container of whatever fertilizer you're using. In some form or other, the word *urea* will likely show up. Nature is organic and uses everything we are made of.

∼

Front and back doors of the dually were open this morning for my canine labor gang to "load up" on their own. They all know that Wednesday is the day I run errands in town. Nike, the new Bluetick rides shotgun, in exactly the same regal hound pose as old Murph, her deceased predecessor, used to take. The order for the passenger upload in the back seat is as follows:

Caesar, the giant Pyrenees/Akbash galoot climbs in first, covering most of the back seat, end to end. Blackie, the old matron mongrel squeezes comfortably into whatever surface space remains in and around Caesar's contour. Blackie is smart enough to know that he's mostly fur anyway. Even grumpy old Spin leaps in, content to recline on the floor behind the drivers seat. Occasionally, during the ride to town and back, Spin will stretch her gray head forward over the console and look up at me, I guess to remind me that she may be ancient but is still alive. Tommy Cat is already perched atop the back seat, licking a paw, and looking out the rear window now and then, guarding our flank.

Of late, Solomon has taken to seeing the canine gang off on these Wednesday mornings. He stands tall, peering into the truck, front and back, perhaps taking a count of the passengers. Sometimes I suspect he's pondering the physical logistics required for him to jump up into the truck. He could easily do it, but what a cacophony would ensue. Might as well toss a water moccasin into the mix. He backs off as doors are closed and proclaims the canine campaign is officially under way by trumpeting a piercing bray to all the world.

In the rearview mirror, I watch the little scamp trot lively back into the horse pasture to join his tall pal Samson for some sweet rye grass. Sol will share all the news of our dog departure with the big guy. I pull up just shy of the length of the wide front gate, put the truck in park, and step down to swing the gate aside for our exit. I repeat the exercise, in reverse, once on the other side of the farm's portal. The dogs watch these maneuvers with great interest, quite willing to get out and assist me if only asked.

On the way to town, I stop on the shoulder, just before the Civilian Conservation Corps-era bridge that crosses the narrow Caterpillar Creek. At the corner of the overgrown lot that borders the creek, I approach the tragic old swayback horse, which stretches over the rusted fence to greet me. Wide-eyed, the grand old whiskered head bobs slowly up and down, happy to see me. Horses are herd animals and need companionship. This miserable creature stands in this same corner every day, all day, just to catch glimpses of passing vehicles. Sometimes he's rewarded with the sight of another horsehead looking back at him from the cozy confines of a shiny trailer.

Like magic, I produce a big red apple from my pocket. The old boy salivates, smiling broadly at me with what remain of his untended large yellow teeth. Nostrils flared in anticipation, he projects those big incisors out to the bright red treasure and proceeds to bite the sweet orb with the delicate touch of a jeweler. I cup the apple for him with my palm so that his old, whiskered lips trust that the precious fruit will not fall away. He's savoring every edge, every newly tooth-carved plane of the apple's surface. His long, handsome eyelashes blink slowly, contentedly, as he chews with the patience of Job. Apple juice flows over his old lips.

Finished with the feast, he leans over the fence toward me, raising his big head slightly, eager for a long-needed chin scratch from a human hand. I linger a bit, gently rubbing one ear. He's calm and getting a little sleepy. I don't want his old frame to fall, so I step closer into the fence while gently sliding my hand off his ear to apply a long, slow stroke down the full length of his hairy neck. He chuffs contentedly, and I promise him that we'll stop again next Wednesday for another chat.

~

Turning into the drive thru lane at Elysia's First National Bank, all the dogs sit up, noses aimed at the tellers' large window. Ellie grins at the dogs through the glass while holding up dog biscuits so they can see. Whining ensues, dog heads extended outside the truck toward Ellie. The wide teller's tray slides within reach of the driver's window. I retrieve dog biscuits for the gang, plus a small plastic bag with a few kitty kibbles. Each dog waits its turn for a biscuit. Tommy Cat climbs up onto the console, watching closely as I arrange the several kibble bits before him.

Critters' needs taken care of, it's my turn. I slide my deposit into the tray and push it closed. It's a sizeable check, the first third of a new commission—a painting for a large lobby of a big title company in Dallas. The theme is a placid evening street scene of several 1930s-era bungalows with fireflies. The wide painting will be five by twelve feet.

Greer's Grocery is never crowded on Wednesdays. All the sales run Thursday through Sunday. It's a cool morning, but I leave the windows part way down so dog heads can stick out and smell the air if desired. Most of the gang will sleep right through my brief absence from the cab. I'm buying basics: a pot-roast for the weekend, cereals, milk, juices, sandwich fixings, and soft drinks for my teen farm workers. My own vegetable gardens and hens supply the rest.

I enjoy chatting with the Greer brothers. There are three of them, about a year apart in age. The three butchers keep themselves on a consistent rotating schedule so that there's always two of them behind the counter. Their father and his twin opened the store long ago and trained the boys how to be butchers and how to manage the store. They always kindly throw in some tasty bones for my canine crew. The dogs watch closely through the back window as I store all the bags into the big cooler (with ice packs) in the bed of the truck.

Next stop, the feed store. We park by the front doors. I see that Pete has already stacked my order on one of the wood pallets lining the dock. Today we're getting a couple of bags of alfalfa cubes for the horses, sweet feed for the cows, dog and cat food for some of the most expensive livestock on the place, organic electrolytes for the hens, and a box of three-inch deck screws.

It's past lunchtime by now, so young Bert's already started his afternoon work-study shift. He comes out to greet us, scratching each pet's head through the open windows, and calling them by name. Bert is a good, hardworking kid. Penny, the co-owner, follows close behind, a Tupper Ware bowl in hand. The dogs' maniacally wagging tails are loudly beating holes in the truck seats. Though they've already assumed the position, Penny tells each one in their turn to sit as she first holds one dog biscuit visibly against her chest, then offers the gift, hand to muzzle. Pete and I chat about the weather while Bert loads my order into the bed of the truck.

Our last stop before heading home is the post office to pick up a carton of new heritage breed chicks that have just arrived. I always take a moment to pause and admire the handsome 1940 mural of a Barnes County landscape. Painted by a follower of famed Texas artist Jerry Bywaters, the scene depicts a farmer and his mule amidst rows of green cotton, looking back toward a small farmhouse silhouetted against a blazing sunset.

My art reverie is interrupted by the exuberantly noisy peeps of dozens of baby chicks I hear behind the rows of ancient post office boxes. I lean over the counter and see a bunch of the yellow feather-balls pecking about on the top of a stainless-steel table. To the delight of the staff, their little beaks make light pinging sounds on the metal surface. Playing awhile with the chicks has become a bit of a tradition at the post office and reminds younger clerks that Elysia is still largely a farming town.

As the cute chicks are returned to their ventilated cardboard containers, I call John, the postmaster, over to the counter. He's been a main fixture in all Elysia's comings and goings for decades, always with a smile. He extends his hand, warmly.

"Hey, Sam. Good to see you." Motioning with a thumb thrown over his shoulder in the direction of the baby chicks, he adds, "We'll have your livestock rounded up soon."

"Good afternoon, John. Sorry my poultry gangsters have distracted the workers."

"The chicks are always good for morale. I figure it's a team-building exercise."

"John. A question. You know that old farm property at the Caterpillar Creek bridge on the way into town?"

John pictures the location in his head.

"Yeah. North-side or south of the County Road?"

"North. It borders the east side of the creek. Who owns that, do you know?"

∾

Visiting artist friends from Ravenna, Italy, recently commented on the *buona fortuna* heaped upon me in the form of a small, but prodigious peach orchard on my farm. They said it must be a gift from *Tellus Mater*, the Roman Goddess (Mother Earth). Having only bought this property near Elysia a few years ago, I didn't plant the prodigious Loring and Hal-Berta peach trees originally. But I am certainly the grateful recipient of their ten-to-twelve-year maturity.

My friends hail from a province famous for peaches, in the north-east of Italy, abutting the Adriatic Sea. Ravenna is one of my favorite towns, boasting churches built in the sixth century by the Byzantine Emperor Justinian and Empress Theodora. These churches are chockful of breathtaking mosaics, including images of blossoming fruit trees. I'd toured those very mosaics with my farm guests, young painters, who I got to know during a mid-career sabbatical to Northern Italy.

My delightfully expressive visitors regaled me with enthusiastic assurances that, indeed, peach trees originated in Ravenna. I didn't argue or counter that the peach probably first arrived in Italy via Greece, and those Greek peaches most likely originated in Persia or China, long before the Trojan War.

During their spring visit, the oldest Loring Peach tree put on quite a show of color for the admiring Italian and Texas artists alike. The tree was powdered all over in bright pink blossoms one dew-sparkled morning. The raking light of sunrise pronounced the contrast of the tree's gnarled black bark trunk against the patches of the flowers. For a long time, those old, twisted branches have contorted themselves to reach around each other in pursuit of sunlight for their infant leaves, not unlike their nearby post oak distant cousins.

The lovely blossoming image gave us all pause. Like a Greek chorus, we all said in unison, "Van Gogh." My Loring and Hal-Berta peach trees in bloom always remind me of some of my favorite Van Gogh paintings: peach trees, pear trees, and almond trees in blossom near Arles, France. He painted the last almond tree just days before his death in 1890, by his own hand with pistol, in the middle of a remote wheat field. Van Gogh was distraught. As he noted in his journal, the recent birth of a son to his brother, Theo, meant that now his brother and sister-in-law would have two dependents to care for, the new baby and Vincent himself. His guilt was unbearable.

His loving brother supported Van Gogh for all the artists' ten-year painting career. Save one, perhaps, none of Van Gogh's nine hundred paintings sold in his lifetime.

Some were displayed in the Paris gallery managed by Theo. It was Theo who introduced his brother to another artist represented by his gallery, the already respected Paul Gauguin. Theo and his wife kept his brother's works in their home, walls covered to the rafters. One year, Van Gogh painted almost two hundred pictures. The tenderness of the last peach-tree and almond tree paintings surely reflect Vincent's attempt at a loving expression of both gratitude and concern for his generous and ever-supportive brother, Theo.

My friends from Ravenna are all young painters trying to perfect realistic still-life in the manner of nineteenth-century American artists. During their stay, I took them to the Amon Carter Museum in Fort Worth so they could study three instructive paintings: William McCloskey's 1889 *Wrapped Oranges*, De Scott Evans' 1888 *Free Sample, Try One*, and Raphaelle Peale's 1813 *Peaches and Grapes in a Chinese Export Basket*. Over my two decades of teaching, I've taken a couple of hundred painting students to see these three American masterworks, up close and personal. Jaws drop in wonder, and in envy. We all sketched and painted bowls of oranges when we got back to the farm.

Our week-long mutual passion for peaches, still-life painting, and Van Gogh having been exhausted, I bade *buona fortuna* to my friends from Ravenna. I think they left a bit perplexed about my decision to pursue a two-pronged path into the future as both an artist and farmer. A part of me envied their certainty in life's purpose as they returned to their art studios by the Adriatic Sea. Youth sometimes has the clearest vision in a straight line from point A to B.

Earlier today, near my own splendid peach tree in blossom, I mixed a less-than-fragrant spring brew of organic fertilizer to be spread over some of the new herb plants. My garden labor was accompanied by the sounds of a family of doves cooing to each other in the early morning air. Not the equally resonant afternoon mourning lament of the dove, but that wonderful wake-up cooing sound, a kind of deep-throated trill of pleasure in the day's beginning.

Occasionally, a young urban art student will ask how anyone (meaning me, their teacher) could shoot a dove. Justifying my own teenage bird hunts to students as candidly as possible, I tried to explain how dove and quail provided protein for many a sharecropper's family supper.

As teens, my cousin Cody and I ate a lot of dove with our families in the late summertime. On his grandfather's big farm outside Hubbard, Texas, we enjoyed rural adventures that Mark Twain's Huck Finn and Tom Sawyer would have shared. We provided minimal farm labor those summers, except for a few monotonous, gnat-infested early mornings hoeing tall, razor-sharp johnsongrass out of the young cotton rows.

In the early mornings we fished in one of two big tanks on the farm. Developers today would refer to each as a "large, scenic lake." For some of the best young excavation equipment talents now, the term seems to be "pool." Whatever the current word, I was famous for having delivered the largest bass ever caught from either of these tanks. Not all family members will support this claim, but Cody's granddad said so, and that's gospel to me.

Returning about midday to the farmhouse, we proudly held up our hefty catches, which dripped tank-water profusely on the back porch. Cody's grandmother always had a word of praise, clasping her hands before her. She would clean them herself before suppertime. A grand farm cook, she knew that cleaning and filleting fresh bass could not be left to the clumsy hands of teenage boys.

"Dinner" for the evening meal, and "Lunch" for noon were cosmopolitan terms I never heard till college, by the way. Growing up, we had "dinner" at midday and "supper" at dusk. Breakfast was at sunrise or before. I'm not sure I could have pronounced the word "brunch" as a child, much less understood the concept.

In late summer, on long-shadowed afternoons, nephews and uncles, empty shotguns lolling at the elbow, would bring home a mess of dove. We boys did pluck the dove feathers, clumsy fingers and all. Supper meant platters heaped with crispy fried smallmouth bass and dove breasts. So, yes, I have a mixture of pleasurable responses when I hear cooing doves in the morning.

After a time of joyous laughter, and tall tales of Hill County adventures around the supper table with our World War II vet uncles and one World War I "doughboy" grandad, bedtime called. Cody and I slept on army-cots out on the big screened-in front porch, where there was always a breeze in late summer evenings. The dark night brought lush wafts of fragrant air from the orchard of ripening peach and pear trees nearby in the dark surround. Sometimes a soft rain would fall on the corrugated tin roof, lulling us to sleep with its gentle, rhythmic patter.

The cool front that blew in recently was a pleasant reprieve for humans and animals at the farm. May seemed to be ending on a warm note, so the slight chill in the air was a kind reminder that summer had not arrived just yet. I was on my way down to the barn at about 5:00 that morning, just for a quick look at Blaze, the orange colt, before I headed off for class. Though retired, I occasionally sub at the college when needed. I'd be teaching a drawing class, since my old friend Suzie had jury duty. I was looking forward to it. Teaching people how to draw is very rewarding, for students and for the instructor.

Looking up from under the bois d'arc canopy of old trees, the spaces of the eastern sky between the leafless branches were speckled with tiny bright white star-flecks. The sky across the west was solid black, covered with dark, cold clouds. I've put that in the memory bank for a future night painting. I've been getting significant commissions for large paintings in commercial spaces—lobby's, conference rooms, and the like. My translucent paintings of evening and night sky landscapes with fireflies have sold well.

The bois d'arc "grove" as I call it is actually a thick stand of aged trees, mostly bois d'arc, but a few tall pecans, and a couple of pesky locusts. Over the years since buying this acreage, I've cleared, trimmed, shaped, and bush-hogged various horse trails and hiking/biking paths through the numerous woods at the farm. A couple of my high school hires ride their trailbikes to work, just so they can head off down one or two of the shaded, twisting lanes on their breaks. Between horses, hikers, and bikers, the paths stay pretty smooth. On winter nights, the compact ground here is like a patch-work quilt of light and dark because of the bare trees.

I'm convinced, by the way, that the black locust tree could not possibly have been in the Garden of Eden. In fact, I'm thinking it was probably the first tree that poor naked Adam and Eve ran into upon expulsion from the garden. If, upon turning away from the closed garden gate, they first had to clear a path through locust trees, then their remorse was tenfold.

Wear armor whenever you are in near vicinity of this tree-beast. Cans of flat-fix, duct-taped to the inside of your tractor fenders is a wise time-saving move. Flesh and tires are no match for the wily locust thorn.

I arrived at the quiet barn, where no tenants were stirring yet. I peered over the rail into Blaze's stall. He was sound asleep in his usual fashion: flat-out. I've never seen a horse sleep so horizontal. His closed eyes display the longest lashes, like a fifties' Hollywood starlet. Blaze's sleeping posture gives no indication of his true awake self's demeanor, especially when in the rambunctious company of his donkey pal, Solomon.

I have seen Blaze stand with hind legs straddling a barn-cart shaft, with one front hoof in a feed bucket, while his pretty head is simultaneously sniffling the steering wheel of the Kubota for errant oat crumbs or alfalfa residue. He is truly a contortionist. And heaven help you trying to do any barn repairs with this curious colt in the vicinity of any job at hand. You can count on Blaze being right there, supervising, literally over your shoulder. Thank heavens he doesn't have opposable thumbs.

His running mate, Sol, is older, but enjoys getting into trouble. And Blaze is never far behind when Sol finds trouble to get into. The only job Sol takes halfway seriously now is his role as shepherd to the Tunis lambs and ewes. But it seems that anywhere beyond the sheep pasture perimeter, Sol's brain jerks into "teenage" gear.

The cute donkey is actually the most popular critter on the farm amongst our many visitors, children and adults alike. Sadly, Solomon has figured this out, and has come to reason that his cuteness can get him out of any jam. My teen helper of few words, Vern, initially questioned the practicality of my "asinine" purchase, commenting, "I don't get it, Sam. You can't milk him, and you can't eat him. What's his purpose?"

I mumbled that "...maybe he'll work as a coyote guard when he grows up." That feeble theory took some time to pan out, but he seems to be adjusting well, at least when in the pasture with the sheep and his working partner, big Caesar, the Pyrenees guard dog.

Sometimes Solomon proudly raises all of his twenty-seven-inch height up on his hind legs, as if he imagines himself a western movie stallion, and nips Blaze at all quarters. Well, truth be told, he was the only stud in the stable until fairly recently. Nevertheless, he is forever by Blaze's side, when not tending to sheep. He's decided that because Blaze's favorite food is hay, he's pretty much done with sweet mix too. Prefers the strong stuff. Blaze's contortionist career serves him well as he now must often straddle Sol, happily eating hay while literally under foot.

Occasionally, if he's outworn his welcome, Blaze will pretend-bite him on the back and flatten him out with the weight of his long head. But mostly he seems contented to graze with him, run and play with him, and scratch Sol's withers gently with his big horse-teeth when asked.

Blaze, the young quarter horse, has impressive conformation, save one big drawback. Clara is chomping at the bit to train him herself. But there's a well-known wrangler up in Montague County that would like that job, after Blaze is a bit older. The colt has a distinct white flame between his huge dark eyes, hence his name. The mark looks hand painted. Sadly, for some viewers, Blaze is just too orange. I mean, he's as vivid as a Whataburger stand. He'll lose points at halter, but that wrangler might make a good roping horse out of him. Besides, I don't mind him being orange, and his equine corral mates don't see that color anyway.

~

Sometimes, right out of the blue, a more contemplative part of my busy brain tells me to turn off the tractor and just breathe in silence for a few moments. It happened this morning at the farm as I was mowing along the fence line of the front horse pasture, up by the county road. A neighbor recently lost a half-acre of new hay due to a lit cigarette butt being casually tossed from a driver's open window. So I'm trying to keep the fire-fuel at a crew-cut level. Though it was early in the day, there was no dew this morning, so the grass mowed easily. Too early for the school bus or delivery trucks, the road was void of whining tires or loud exhausts.

It was a clear sky all the way up to the hazy contour line of the distant Ouachita mountains, just north of the Red River. Birds were singing and chirping around me. I found my neck and shoulders relaxing. My hands hung beside me at the ends of their arms, instead of gripping the steering wheel with determination. The tractor was in neutral, and I let my brain slide into that position as well.

I was entertained a good while by a handsome red-winged blackbird, one of my favorite Texas birds. He had spent much of the morning flitting about from atop one of the compost piles, with many return trips to the lower branches of a nearby fat juniper. Hopefully there's a nest in there somewhere, and the male was bringing home the bacon (bugs, in this case). Normally the red-wings would have their woven cup-like nest attached to reeds or thick grass, but this summer has required close scalping in some areas, because of those not-too-distant wildfires. So the parents have probably sought slightly higher ground in the shelter of the juniper.

The male red-winged blackbird is a striking creature. Avid bird-watchers must surely admire his perfect proportions and densely consistent black coat. The epaulets on his shoulders are bright red patches, trimmed in yellow, that project vividly toward the eye, placed strategically as they are against a solid black field of feathers. The bright red patches on coal-black wings are spectacular examples of nature's design team. His distinctive beak and legs are pure steel gray.

I like to draw this blackbird with soft 7B graphite lead, and multiple layers of waxy colored pencil on white Stonehenge all-cotton paper.

Done with the mowing, I returned the tractor to the shed. I decided to walk up to the herb garden on the hill, trying to hold onto my peaceful sunrise interlude. I wanted to be "mindful of the moment," as my lovely sidekick Annie would say. As I started up the road, I was joined by my pals, who seemed to saunter up from all directions: Blackie, the mongrel-breed, Caesar, the Pyrenees/Akbash mix, Nike the Bluetick Coonhound, and Tommy Cat, the feline who thinks he's a dog. Circling about, each managed to touch my hands with cold, moist canine noses. I knew Tommy Cat felt envious, so I reached down to lift him up, carrying him from my hip. He purred contentedly. Often, he likes me to carry him upside down.

We were headed toward the herb garden up on the hill, to see if

the guineas had been doing their job of eating pesky young grasshop-
pers we'd seen recently near the raised beds. Pete at the feedstore had
encouraged me to order a dozen of the famed insect assassins.

Glancing into the old grove of tall, native pecans, I spotted the
highly decorated blackbird, standing tall amidst a huge display of
pink prairie roses. What a sight! I've trained the wild rose to spiral
around the trunk and into the lower branches of a younger pecan
tree in the grove. Maybe the grand fellow was taking a break from
his parental duty as food gatherer on an ever-hotter sunny morning
to seek cooler temps beneath a shady green canopy. In any event,
the scene was worthy of Audubon's brush and watercolors. The
rich, dark contour of the blackbird was distinctly contrasted with
the soft pastel petals of the flowers. The wild rose blooms are
almost daisy-like, open shapes, resembling small, pink windmills.
The black bird's epaulets blazed, even in the splendid bouquet of
flowers.

Armed with my trusted canine companions, I approached the
fenced-in herb garden, crossed the flagstone entry, and stood beneath
the old metal hay-ring that was turned on end last year to create an
arch for the front gate. Wisteria now climbs up its rusted metal frame.
To the chagrin of my pals, I shut the wrought-iron gate behind me,
not allowing them into the garden.

I was stopped in my tracks. The guineas were doing a job all right,
but not the job I had assigned them. All the new Romaine lettuce
heads were sheared down to a few inches height each. Those gorgeous
heads of lettuce were formerly about seven inches tall just days from
being ready for sale at the farmers' market, either as individual
Romaine heads or in a salad mix with leafy greens and arugula. I ran
the guineas out of the lettuce bed and nearly wept. My customers
would be so disappointed. Worse, they wouldn't be handing me
greenbacks for the greens.

I stood amongst the Romaine ruins, stunned that the winged
creatures called guineas had turned on their providers and eaten the
profits. Pete had assured me that their presence in the gardens would
mean fewer bugs. I said I couldn't recall my granny ever having
guineas inside her gardens. The guineas of my youth stayed in the

fields and nearby trees, "sleeping rough," as my Brit students used to say when I taught in Derby, UK.

The pampered Bartlett Farm guineas are accustomed to coming and going as they please, to and from their roosting branches in the post oaks near the fancy Chicken Mansion. They must assume that their current labor contract includes gourmet victuals. Flushing them from the lettuce bed, the guineas simply hopped over to the arugula bed and commenced dining. No respect.

I found myself pondering an important question: could I replace guineas with domesticated roadrunners? We have a resident family of them, in addition to the Red-winged Blackbirds. How thrilled am I, always, to see either momma or poppa roadrunner racing across the garden or nearby pasture, carrying this big tarantula or that question-able-looking snake. Roadrunners aren't interested in my arugula. The buffet they enjoy features big bugs and reptiles. The guineas might soon find themselves "made redundant" as my Derby students would have said.

T he good thing about building a wood barn is that the horses always have something to eat. Wood has lots of cellulose. Plants such as deadly nightshade or lily of the valley some-times show up in a pasture and they are certainly not things you want your horse to eat. Let the horses eat the barn. First, make sure you're not building the barn with treated wood. Then proceed to provide your remuda with the finest cedar battenboard and one-by trim you can afford.

There's lots of prep work going on up at the gardens these days. "Lumberjack" Liz has scheduled a weekend event for her fellow forestry majors from Stephen F. Austin. It's a project that fulfills part of her teaching assistant graduate hours requirement but is mainly a labor of love for her to share a passion for heirloom produce with her friends. There'll be twenty or so grad students, and one or two profs, camping on the rise above the herb gardens for a couple of days.

So, in addition to all the usual harvesting and preparation for weekend markets, farmhands Clara and Vernon (Vern) are spending much of their time on clean-up detail and landscaping.

My sidekick Annie is supervising much of the prep via cellphone, as she won't arrive until Friday afternoon. She's up in Oklahoma City this week, interviewing some farm-to-table chefs for a new food article she's writing. Vern, who thinks she hangs the moon, is dutifully scalping the garden grounds clean of any vegetation Annie finds unsightly. Evidently, we don't want horticulture visitors to see that all our blue-blood organic herbs and heirloom produce have ne'er-do-well weedy relatives living practically next door.

Dignified and costly organic plants such as arugula, salad burnet, chervil, French sorrel, lemon thyme, Florentine fennel, and Greek oregano grow fat and green, perched high up and proud in their pent-house-like raised beds. These are pampered plants, the elite. Annie doesn't want them threatened at the sight of their ugly cousins who, moment by moment, try to scale the walls and break into the elevated mansions of fine families like the Bergamots. Like unwanted in-laws, weeds such as little barley, yellow sweet clover, johnsongrass, prostrate knotweed and mimosa vine are forbidden to show themselves near the approved garden residents.

A lawyer friend once told me he thought that "weeds are just flowers without representation." Maybe that's so. Annie, for example, says all parts of dandelions are edible. She adds the leaves occasionally to our salads and to scrambled eggs.

British artist Edward J. Lowe's nineteenth century drawings and prints of grasses and weeds are magnificent examples of the beauty to be found in those plants "without representation." Lowe's images are precise, linear silhouettes, emphasizing the delicate formations of wild flora, especially the diversity of shapes of the thirty-eight species of ferns in the UK. In his spare time, Lowe was a botanist, meteorologist, and an astronomer—a true student of natural science.

The renaissance German artist, Albrecht Durer, known as the "Leonardo of the North," drew and painted many studies of native flora and fauna during his travels. A single watercolor by Durer, *Tall Grass*, (also titled *The Great Piece of Turf*) has provided countless art history doctoral candidates around the world with a winning topic. It is a richly detailed description of every blade and tendril within Durer's cropped view of a simple tuft of grass in an open field.

During my studio teaching days, I would instruct the occasional fast-on-the-draw student to slow down and copy Durer's microscopic view of a single tuft of grass. "Look before you draw" is always good advice.

If American cowboy-humorist Will Rogers "never met a man he didn't like," then you might say that American wild food advocate Euell Gibbons never met a weed he didn't like. Gibbons' "wild diet" philosophy is periodically rediscovered, newly excavated if you will, on YouTube, where you can find him in an old TV commercial, hawking Grape Nuts cereal. My mother loved Grape Nuts cereal, and she loved to quote Euell Gibbons saying, "Ever eat a pine tree?" I never quite understood how that phrase endeared Mom's generation to eat Grape Nuts.

My longtime artist pal, George Clay, confirms that his mom, too, was a big fan of Gibbons and his "pine tree" motto. George was raised near Lake St. John, Concordia Parish, Louisiana. Foraging for wild edibles has a long history in his family. Wild lowlands flora and fauna are common themes for George's evocative wood sculptures. Years ago, I traded George a painting of fireflies in swamp grass to remind him of home. For me, he carved a magical Jackrabbit-headed walking stick. I never hike without the long-eared fellow.

A hearty and hefty 1968 *New Yorker* article by the Pulitzer Prize winning author John McPhee, titled "A Forager," is a wild food tale that the reader hopes won't end. McPhee's account describes several days' hiking with Euell Gibbons in the immense northern woods near Troxelville, Pennsylvania, then Gibbons' farm home. The two trekkers ate wild food only during the trip. They ate lots of herbs and weeds, including wild ground cherries.

I was pleased to read about the ground cherries, also called "paper-husk tomatoes," as we grow and sell these little delicacies. Resembling a tiny tomatillo in appearance, the little 'tomato' inside the paper shell is sweet and tart, producing a "pop" of citrus flavor in your mouth. Harvesting these gems is a labor-intensive endeavor, but well worth the effort.

Just remember that ground cherries, delights to human palates and health, are poison to horses. Let them eat the barn.

~

L ate in the afternoon on Mother's Day, I was stuck in a sudden noisy downpour of fat rain and hail in the parking lot of Home Depot in Sherman. For about ten minutes, the strong diagonal wind gusted with such force the truck was jostled about. I'd incidentally parked next to a line of crape myrtles planted along the curb, which provided some relief from the blast. In the cab, watching and hearing all those white balls of ice bouncing around felt like I was inside a big concession popcorn machine. But during one very brief pause in the deluge, I could tell from the light around the fringes of the fast-moving storm cloud that the furor would be short-lived. The storm was speedily moving to the east, little funnel-tails of wannabe tornadoes dipping below the long horizontal cloud line.

My mom, rest her soul, would have been terrified had she been in the truck. Her dad's family had survived a terrible Hill County tornado when he was a kid, so my grandfather was especially diligent in getting his own family to safety. Mom grew up on the farm in Irene, often being shook awake with all the other kids during bad weather. Paw Paw, as he was called, feared for himself and his offspring. Little sons and daughters were hauled outside in the middle of the night during a bad storm and wrangled down into the sturdy underground root cellar. During such events, the structure became the "storm cellar." Mom told us how scary it was for her, being huddled with the family in the dark, as the wind above howled and ripped at the house and barns. The family would be soaking wet, having run from house to cellar through a deluge, surrounded by the smells from boxes of onion starters and seed potatoes and the dirt floor of the deep storm cellar. The glass Mason jars of assorted canned goods and pickled items rattled and pinged against each other on rickety shelves as the storm raged above them.

Of course, families in North Central Texas counties are all too familiar with the real dangers posed by tornadic activity. On May 6,

1930, an F4 tornado struck Bynum, jumped to Mertens, hit Frost, then moved on to Ennis. At the end of the storm, forty-one were dead and two hundred injured. Mom and Dad's respective families were on adjacent farms in Irene, so they rushed to help relatives and friends in all those neighboring towns hit by the storm.

Mom often talked of being in Waco when possibly the worst tornado in Texas history fell on the day after Mother's Day, May 11, 1953. Mom and her twin were fabric shopping at Monnig's for a dress they were making for a cousin's wedding. An F5 as recorded by Texas A&M, the tornado was about a third of a mile wide. Mom described it as a straight line, south to north, that ran mercilessly "...right through town." One hundred fourteen people lost their lives and nearly six hundred were injured. With hundreds of homes destroyed, thousands of damaged structures and, as Mom said, "...cars thrown every which-a-way", for her, the memory of the event was a devastating reminder that May storms are not to be ignored.

Much has been written about the more recent tornado of 1957, which hit Dallas. I remember Mom calling my brother and me to look out of a small upstairs bathroom window of our duplex on Edgefield in Oak Cliff. She said, pointing to a V-shaped cloud in the distance, "Boys, that's a tornado." She rushed us downstairs and across the street to an elderly woman's home (Mom was not going to be caught in an upstairs apartment during a tornado). As we stood on the neighbor's front porch, knocking at the door loudly, we could hear the approaching funnel. And it did sound like a locomotive engine.

Our neighbor was hard of hearing, and did not come to the door, so Mom responded to neighbors shouting at us from back across the street who had seen our plight. As we rushed to their little bungalow, I looked up to see the tornado, just at Davis Street, and was momentarily hypnotized, my feet frozen still in the middle of Edgefield.

I recall the vivid sound of stuff falling into the center of the funnel, crashing and breaking glass and metal, lumber, and such. I remember seeing a huge white refrigerator, spun to the outside edge of the thing, suspended for an instant, and then collapsing back into the center. The three of us—my mom, brother and I—wound up in a bathroom with the neighbor family, gathered tightly in a large pink bathtub beneath the cover of a mattress. When the tornado passed, we looked up to see two-by-fours and pieces of metal, which had pierced the ceiling over our heads, and the sky through holes in the roof above.

All the yards along Edgefield were covered in debris, like heaping piles of refuse at a dump. Parents held their children close as they came out to survey the considerable damage. Power lines were down, some of them dancing snake-like, furiously popping with fire every time they struck the street. The thick trunk of an old cottonwood on the corner looked like twisted rope. An old man across the street sat in his front-porch swing, smiling. I'd noticed him sitting there just before the tornado hit. He must have ridden out the storm in that swing and been witness to the whole incredible event. As a kid, I envied his freedom to do that. As an adult, I appreciate my mom helping me develop some common sense over the years, to step aside when in the path of a tornado.

Homer, the blind lamb

FOUR

Summer Shearing and Copperhead Bites

The dogs and I reconnoitered the tanks earlier today (modern excavators call them "lakes"), to see if the dam and surrounding ground is drying up enough for the horses' big feet. The dogs found every nook and cranny still rife with mud. The tanks aren't big. Each is one acre, fifteen feet deep at center. The west tank has a wide spillway which allows easy movement of excess water around the dam and off into a natural gully, channeling the water into Hackberry Creek. The east tank's long drainpipe funnels extra water through the dam into a pretty cascade down to the same creek. If the creek crests, and it does now and then, any extra water eventually drains off to the southeast into a stand of old hardwoods and native pecans.

In the dry season, this is one of the favorite spots for owners to ride their boarded horses. Over the years, I've hacked out quite a level path from the wilderness thicket. Below the dam, the place is quiet, shady, and cool. A respite for the horses after going through their paces across sunny pastures, the grove's dappled sunlight glistens on their wet backs. The Impressionists Renoir and Degas would have painted the scene plein air. Monet would have ignored the horses.

The sounds of the animals' footfalls, occasional whinnies, and the creaking of saddles and shaking of withers all harmonize somehow with the songbirds and doves nesting in the tall trees. It is a natural chorus, lulling horse and rider into a pleasant daze. It's a kind of magical grotto, punctuated with tall tree columns and leafy canopy throughout. It's a space for reflection, not for darting and dashing. Even teen riders slow their mounts to thoughtful walks through the sylvan sanctuary.

Young willows have pretty much taken over the east tank. Tall, aquatic grasses compete, and are welcome, but the thirsty willows quickly spread branches full of leaves to swallow up much of the sunlight before it gets down to the thinner grass. A couple of wet days' work of hand-sawing the pesky things should do the trick. Chain-saws have limited effect under water, by the way.

You have to respect willows. There are two floating willow-leaf formations that pretty much stay stationary on top of the water. I've been admiring the shapes for several days, leading up to my intended removal of same. Yesterday, I noticed lots of vertical shapes rising above the floating leaves. Tommy Cat was beside me, stretching his striped head as far as possible to peer at what I was studying. Upon closer inspection, I was stunned to realize that the new "twigs" were in fact pistils reaching into the light to create new willows. The leaf-flotillas had gathered enough dirt, leaves, and pollen below the surface to establish a hydroponic environment from which to procreate.

The east tank has enough mature small-mouthed bass and blue-gill now to look forward to some fun fishing this summer. Nieces and nephews and neighbors' kids will be well entertained. Tommy Cat, despite thinking he's a dog, cannot help but reveal his true cat nature whenever near swimming creatures. He loves to stand close beside me or between my legs when I toss out a fresh bucket of game-fish pellets onto the surface of the water.

The pellets spread into a wide pattern, determined by the movement of the wind-pushed water. As the food-bits float, the fish rush to the surface, raising their fat heads above the water to gulp down the tasty morsel, often with a big splash. This drives the cat-dog crazy. He is totally hooked on these live fish.

Farmers are never fully satisfied with current weather conditions, no matter how profuse the crop standing before them. During time of gray skies and excess moisture, I try to remind myself that a dry season is surely just around the bend and may come on with ferocity. As the three dogs and I walk the fence line, I pause every half-mile or so to listen to various solar hot-wire chargers around the farm for the distinctive "click" which rhythmically repeats itself, announcing that a consistent, pulsing current is being transmitted all along any connected line. Leave your finger on the wire for a couple of seconds to experience the phenomena. A couple of the solar-panel chargers are not clicking as loudly as usual on this day's inspection. Note the distinction, "solar." We haven't had a lot of solar influence lately hereabouts. If water were charging these panels, we'd have a dangerous electrical field being emitted over the whole property. Even fine horsehair would stand on end. Of late, it's sure easy to see why sun-worship raises its pagan head now and then amongst those who need it most: bikini-clad tan-seekers and straw hat-clad farmers.

I imagine that only a few days after the three dogs and I have completed our inspection of over-flowing tanks and sagging fenceposts, the weather will probably have changed, overnight. The world of Barnes County and environs will have become a vision of the perfect synthesis of light, moisture, and soil that mother earth intended.

Grass will be too tall, too green, and too wet for the horses, and birds will be singing on leaf-filled branches. And impatient landowners, seduced by the glorious sun's appearance, will bravely venture forth where they know they should not go, promptly getting the tractor stuck in mud up to the eyeballs. That's close to being a mixed metaphor, but you know it's what really happens.

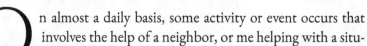

On almost a daily basis, some activity or event occurs that involves the help of a neighbor, or me helping with a situation at their place. These farm-side assistance calls may only take a few minutes, but the immediate dilemma always requires two heads to solve or four hands to complete.

Now that I'm trying my own artist's hand at farming, I'm often reminded of the many parents of friends that I got to know as a child, simply because of mutual neighborly assistance. Farming families are self-reliant, but friends come in handy. Let's say the tractor blows a gasket. The kids are at school. Mom's in town running errands while Dad's thumb gets bit twice by a couple of adolescent copperheads sunbathing on top of the garden gate.

Recently I enjoyed an extended weekend "assistance" visit from my cousin, Harvey, now a successful dog and horse trainer down in Archer County. Harv visits a couple of times a year, and he usually brings his teenage kids, Angie and Andy. Assorted horses and dogs often tag along, and I suspect the critters' inclusion is usually part of some training exercise.

On a splendid Friday in June, Harvey had brought his big Farmall tractor and disk-rig to help prepare some acreage on the farm for re-seeding native prairie grasses. I needed to replenish what was lost when dams were formed for the new one-acre tanks that were excavated last summer.

With help and advice from the Natural Resources Conservation Service (NRCS) and the Noble Foundation, the Tunis sheep would be grazing on organic native grass in a few years. Harv also brought his fancy sheep dog, Moses, just to show me what a real dog could do with sheep.

Harv did a great job of disking some long neglected acreage. Other than getting stuck once and the kids spending hours chiseling hard-ened clay off the disks, the whole disking and planting process went well that weekend. I borrowed an ancient metal harrow from a friend, Jimmy, up the road. It was easily attached to my little thirty-horse-power Kubota's three-point, and the old, rusty harrow performed grandly, creating perfect shallow channels for the new seed.

The day after the planting had started off with a promising soft morning rain, which turned into a deluge that evening. In my mind's eye, I pictured all the new native prairie grass seed washing off down into the adjacent gullies and Hackberry Creek. But nature obliged after all. Weeks later, Annie and I, along with farmhand Clara, were ecstatic to see various new sprouts of grass popping up. Despite the repeated downpours, the grass had secured its footing, and would soon display a beautiful ten acres of restored native prairie. The pasture preparation had taken about a day and a half. We celebrated by driving into Elysia that night for pizza.

The next day, Harv proudly brought forth Kit Carson, his prize sheep dog, to load up one of our rams he was borrowing. Kit did a good job of helping us cram a fat ram into a large dog-training crate. Little did we know a battle not unlike the gunfight at the OK Corral was about to ensue.

As further demonstration of Kit's intelligence and agility, Harvey ordered his confident canine to "...send up the sheep." Kit dutifully got the sheep running and then directed them into more or less of a straight line up the hill from the barn toward the house. We were impressed, since we sometimes find our sheep wandering hither and yon, even into the feed room, when we, or guests, have left a gate open.

The idea of being able to impose order on a farm's animal community is something we sadly have accepted as having only been achieved by Noah and his family long ago.

The sheep huddled together, cowered by the authority of Kit. Then, at once, responding immediately to Harv's signal, Kit ordered the sheep to "move out" and hustled them back down the hill.

The sheep obeyed, and were brought to a fence corner, back near the barn. Kit proudly crouched down in the deep rye grass, one eye on the corralled sheep, one eye on Harvey.

The other set of observant eyes belonged to Solomon, our minia-ture Sicilian donkey. With ever more intense concentration, he had been studying Kit's every move. He is a courteous host but takes his perceived job as boss of the farm very seriously.

Sol welcomes all visitors, two-legged and four-legged alike, usually with a nod and a hug. He looks you in the eye, to take measure of your grit, no doubt.

But unbeknownst to us, Sol had now decided enough was enough, Kit-wise. In the blink of an eye, the little equine positioned himself between the trembling sheep and Kit, the wonder dog, who seemed confused. He barked at the little ass, but to no avail. He looked to Harv for directions. Harv, at first, laughed at the impertinence of little donkey Sol, and signaled Kit to move the sheep.

The champion dog stood up, and advanced. Sol raised a small front hoof and stomped at the dog, clipping its erect ear. Kit backed off. Sol turned his rear on the dog and kicked high in the air with both rear feet, a warning to stay away. Solomon turned his full side toward the sheep and actually leaned into the cornered flock, pressing his little body into theirs. He glared at Kit, as if to say, "These are *my* sheep." As the stomping defense was repeated, we all got a good demonstration of Sol's substantial skills at dealing with interlopers and predators.

After the dust had settled, Harvey tried to make the best of the situation. He confided to me that he had to choose between letting Kit be ruined as a sheepdog by a jackass, or let Sol have his day. He decided to have the humbled dog "load up" into his truck. Later that night, Sol got an extra handful of sweet feed, and a well-earned brushdown, having finally grown into the shepherd's role for which he was originally hired.

Texas summers are stressful on sheep. Our heritage breed Tunis sheep up here in Barnes County usually get sheared in May, early or late, depending on summer heat forecasts and on the availability of our shearer, Lucky Thomas. He's a tall, strong fellow in his twenties. Lucky has no trouble upending a big ewe and having her back pressed against his chest in one fell swoop. Off their feet, sheep are pretty docile. Lucky is a master shearer, efficient, and rarely makes a nick. Annie can't stand to watch a sheep get sheared, even by Lucky. She doesn't like to hear their bleating during Lucky's visits, so she stays in the house with the radio on.

A couple of lambs were born on April Fool's Day this year. Tunis lambs are red all over, a kind of burnt sienna. It's as if someone's dusted every inch of the little things with cinnamon, head to hoof. In adults, the wool becomes an ecru color, but they retain red faces and legs. The first Tunis ewes and lambs I bought were from a breeder out east, near Ladonia. As we were closely observing a small flock jostling around trying to get back to the barn, one small lamb went on the wrong side of the gate from his mother. They traipsed along several yards, Mom on one side, baby on the other side of the fence.

"Oh, Lord," said the breeder. "I call that one Numbskull. He is *not* bright, and he's constantly losing his Mother." The ewe retraced her steps back around gate and fence to round up the bleating lost boy. "Tell you what...," said the owner. "If you'll buy the ewe, I'll throw in Numbskull for free...if you want him."

I drove the sheep home, certain that I was *not* going to call that cute little guy "Numbskull."

The little red lamb did sometimes get turned around in a directly opposite direction from his Mom. He often wound up on the opposite side of the fence from her, particularly when all the flock were racing in from pasture at supper time. I observed him as often as I could over several days.

At first, I thought maybe he didn't hear well, but he usually seemed to locate her by the vocal admonitions she'd yell his way. He bumped into things, I noticed, when on his own. He sometimes bumped into me and would bleat with his noggin pressed against my leg. I began petting his head and withers to calm him down. Eventually I figured out that the lamb was almost blind.

Vet John said he probably could see shapes, maybe lights and darks, but no details and no sense of distance or depth perception. Soon the little guy followed the sound of my own voice as much as his mother's. He was smart. He was curious and engaging. He just couldn't see. That's why I named him after Homer, the blind poet.

July has been particularly blistering this summer. We've hit several weeks of little or no rain—and even with us so near the Red River. If rain is in the air, as clouds often form along its path, we usually get some benefit from the proximity. I'm speaking of the Red River that divides Texas and Oklahoma, of course, not the one that divides North Dakota and Minnesota.

July heat brings joy along with the pain, however. Some plants adore the heat. All the plants enjoy the morning summer temps and sunlight. But the late afternoon sun is relentless. Don't be alarmed if everything in your garden is drooping a bit from the ultimate interrogation lamp. Basil, arugula, and sage will sag pitifully, as if to say, "That's it. I'm done. Just shoot me." But it will be back next morning, especially with if a little dew quenches its thirst overnight.

Many years ago, we made our first trip up near Bolton, North Carolina, to visit extended family.

Our lively and fun distant cousins farm huge crops of peanuts and beans up there. All the talk that early summer was about the woes of practicing dryland farming in the Carolinas. I heard the term used in almost every conversation. Even with their farm's close proximity to the Atlantic ocean (I'd say a stone's throw away), the family started every meal's grace with a plea for rain.

I was up at dawn on the first morning of our visit, watching the sun come up over the nearby ocean. Standing on the front porch steps, I was enjoying a cup of hot coffee. Slowly, I became aware of soft drips of water occasionally falling on me as dew slid down from the standing-seam metal roof above. I looked upon a huge and handsome field of beans that reached out to the horizon. It was a large, well-fed landscape, a whole field of tall green plants bathed in dew, glistening like holiday lights.

Over breakfast that morning, my cousin began saying grace with a request for rain. As the meal ensued, I couldn't help but offer up a lecture for the family, clarifying the definition of the term "dryland farming." That term apparently has a whole different meaning in Texas compared to North Carolina. I invited them all to come to Barnes County if they wanted to see genuine dryland farming.

The scorching, raking sunlight of afternoon and evening can be minimized with a little planning. Especially if you're doing backyard gardening with only a few raised beds. Ten-by-ten-foot square tents are inexpensive and provide a good amount of shade, providing you're attentive and able to move the tent at least once during the afternoon. Shortly after noon, you can pop up the tent and move it to direct the shade where you want it. Remember to secure at least two of the feet in case a big wind suddenly blows through. Nine-foot patio umbrellas are ideal for small, raised beds, and more easily moved.

It's true that gardeners and farmers have to be frugal and accurate with their watering system during this time of the year, to keep plants alive and productive. It means many absurdly early mornings or late evenings making sure every drop of moisture is put to best use in the coolest parts of the day.

There just aren't enough *Diviners* around anymore.

My mom's Uncle Cecil was also her godfather, and he was a respected diviner. Her middle name was Cecil, given to her at birth to honor the man. He was an excellent farmer, with a glorious garden out back of their little farmhouse in what is now downtown Frisco. Mom adored Uncle Cecil, so I remember him well from my childhood visits, and lessons learned in his big garden.

Uncle Cecil could find water. If you were going to dig a well in North Texas, you consulted him about signs and conditions to look for. If you farmed in Denton or Collin County, you might be fortunate enough to have the man come himself to locate water for you. He found hidden springs and wells with a forked, V-shaped willow, peach, or witch hazel divining rod.

The Irish Poet, and Nobel Laureate, Seamus Heaney (1939-2013) wrote about someone of Uncle Cecil's talents in an early published poem titled "The Diviner." In the middle stanza of the poem, Heaney describes the purpose, action, and outcome of divining. The unnamed Irish diviner in the poem goes through the same gestures and method used by our Texas diviner.

"The Diviner" is a favorite poem of mine, so naturally I eagerly discussed it with faculty and students during the year I taught in the UK on a teacher exchange. The argument I made compared respective difficulties likely to be encountered by a diviner finding water in Ireland or England, compared with a diviner finding water in West Texas. I'd say Uncle Cecil wins that contest.

The old well on my place dried up long before I arrived on the scene. Some folks have encouraged me to bite the bullet and drill for water. That's an expensive proposition, especially since the farm already had a water hookup to the local water co-op. José Cantu and I laid considerable extra lines for the new organic gardens and henhouses, but the lines for house and barn were already done. My first year on the farm, we installed no lead, frost-proof faucets for all the exposed hydrants. To remove chlorine and other unwanted chemicals, we maintain filters on all the water used for the organic herb and produce gardens, and the melon patches. This decision turned out to be a wise one, especially for marketing purposes to chefs.

But many things in the garden actually relish the hot temperature and hot light of an unclouded sun. Our garden abounds with certain glorious herbs and produce right now. The unusual round lemon cucumber plants, with broad, bright green leaves, have climbed to the top of the long, curved hog-panel brace I installed for them. The fat pickling cukes are already mature and ready for the dill, lush with seed-heads, from another bed.

In a different part of the garden, several beds are chock-full of spotted yellow and green leaves and thick vines of the Moon and Stars watermelons; likewise for the Black Diamonds and green-flesh honeydews in other beds. The sight of lots of yellow flowers means lots of luscious melons. Melons like plenty of sun and water. Watermelon flowers are edible, and like pumpkin or squash blossoms can be battered and fried.

Granny loved honeydews. But the melon loyalty expressed by us kids was always extended to the lush red sweetness of a hefty watermelon, chilled in a washtub full of ice.

The dark-green zucchinis are just reaching their max and are still covered with huge, gorgeous blossoms of a bright yellow-orange tint. This year, in the dappled shade of filtered afternoon sun, provided by a large juniper I've trimmed way up, Annie has arranged dozens of terracotta pots in a curved line. A bed of curly leaf parsley parallels the same curved contour line. The terracotta pots are brimming with colorful, and edible, nasturtium blooms. The natural scene seems to mimic Monet's thousands of daubs of paint colors.

The oak-leaf lettuce has finally bolted. Spinach is done for. The carrots are making their last hurrah. But the second crop of olive-shaped radishes will be ready soon (the greens are as good as the radish itself). Grown in the coolness of spring, the first crop had little heat. These will be hotter on the palate. The contrast of the cool texture and fiery bite of a summer radish is delightful. In the spring, we'll be selling French breakfast radishes, the long, elegant looking crucifers. I imagine these beauties are what Cleopatra served Mark Antony during their courtship. A market customer of ours, who moved to Texas from Maine for a temporary job thirty years ago, swears the only proper way to eat French breakfast radish is with fresh local butter and fleur de sel.

Beets are also cruciferous plants, but they do best in North Texas in the fall and spring. We love the bold taste, shape, and vibrant color of Bull's Blood beets. Sliced, the gorgeous red disks feature concentric circles, like tree rings. Annie loves to add the curly red leaf-tops to green spring salads with walnuts and gorgonzola crumbles. The rich taste of organic beets will have to wait for cooler weather now.

But the playful running branches of the season's cherry-husk tomatoes hang heavy with hundreds of delicate, delicious gems of fruit, available only in the very hottest part of summer. Also called ground cherries, and related to tomatillos, the little fruit is packaged by nature in a delicate paper-husk cover. The taste of the tiny grape is more tropical than tomato, with a slight reminder of pineapple on the taste buds. Harvesting the little golden gems is a bit tedious (and hard on the knees), but easily retrieved by the small hands and fingers of your youngest farm family workers. One of our top chefs removes the paper-thin husks, dipping the little fruits into a hot sugar bath so that they cool into a thin candy-coated treat.

≈

Last week, I turned the battered but trusty 1992 Isuzu Rodeo out of the half-acre watermelon patch up onto the raised dam road. Creating the road across the top of the dam was a laborious, but necessary endeavor. We laid it between the recently excavated east tank and the steep ravine down into the natural run-off toward Hackberry Creek, twenty feet below the dam. I stopped to open the ten-foot metal gate which kept the horses in their pasture at the front of the property and out of the herbs and produce gardens up the hill. I always made this little journey on Thursdays over the dam to check on erosion, willow tree invasion, and beaver damage.

The long gate swung easily downhill. Peering over the lip of the ravine, I gasped at the bountiful sight below. Covering at least a 1200-square-foot area, large cantaloupes clung to the steep incline. The near volleyball-sized golden yellow orbs glowed brightly within the surrounding green mélange of wild ground cover and sticky-vine. I figured a hundred or more gorgeous melons lay right there just below my feet.

Involuntarily, I pulled off my old straw hat and scratched my sweaty head, bemused by this unplanned harvest gift. I surmised that coyotes (or horses), or my own farm dogs must have hauled off bits and pieces of last year's melon crop and slopped remains off down the steep hill. No way could birds have been responsible for transferring this many seeds.

I grinned at the sight of such good fortune, filled with a sense of gratitude for nature's generous surprises. At Saturday's farmers market in Sherman, these fat melons would command four dollars apiece. I could be looking at six hundred dollars or more, as my wide eyes searched further down the dam's wall, discovering more and more yellow balls of gold. Even with my slow math mind, I calculated that this bountiful, wild crop would considerably make up for last year's horrid loss of eighty beautiful Black Mountain watermelons. A huge pack of coyotes had ventured out of their thicket-dens along the nearly dried-up creek, looking for anything with moisture inside. Desperately, dangerously, their communal thirst had driven them to bust open the life-saving watermelons in the middle of the day. Mother Nature may have played a role in their survival by keeping me away most of that day, picking up a flatbed load of hay near Bowie.

Repelling a few feet down the slope, I lifted one of the cantaloupes, pressed the end opposite the stem for stretch, smelled the ripe skin, and knew these babies were ready for harvest. How they grew so fat in the shade of all the hardwoods along the creek and dam became a topic of much discussion at the market, and amongst my farm neighbors. I climbed back up to the Rodeo and grabbed my cell-phone off the dashboard. The nearby Elysia High School ag instructor answered the call on the other end.

"Angus!" I shouted into the phone (reception was wretched on the farm some days). "I could sure use a couple of kids this afternoon to pick some ripe melons, asap." Angus answered, "Well, Christie is here helping me get ready for the weekend plant sale. Maybe she can find another student to help her pick the melons later today."

"Put her on the phone, please." Christie was a junior whose family farmed a few miles from my place, though her parents both worked day jobs in town. She had grown up helping out at their farm and was like a member of the family to me and Annie. But we tried not to ask her to work much during the school year, as she was a star member of the Elysia track team and on her way to college scholarships.

"Christie," I said, "It's Sam. I need your help. I've got some melons ready for market that I didn't expect. Need picking today. Can you round up another student to harvest them?"

"Yes, sir. I'll get Megan to help. She's been pricing new running shoes, so can use the cash. Probably can't get there 'til 5:30, OK?"

"That's fine. Thanks a million." I answered happily, confident that the melons would be picked properly and stored carefully by Christie for the market on Saturday. She understood the importance of the surprise crop of melons, as she had often helped me in a pinch since I first started selling the herbs and produce. It was a good thing I'd have a couple of track stars helping me harvest the surprise crop. Their calves would get a good workout, picking cantaloupes on a steep slope of sticky-vine. Christie, a future botanist, would photo-graph the site, for sure. It was certainly the strangest melon patch any of us had seen before. At least we'd all be harvesting in the shade.

Spin, the blue heeler

FIVE

Prayers and Prairie Fires

Vern Taylor is a man of few words. He is a young man of few words, maybe sixteen going on seventeen. His dad, Garland, is an outgoing guy, a "hail fellow well met." He's a respected member of our rural volunteer fire department. Everybody calls him G.T. He trains hunting dogs. Louisiana Catahoula Cow Hog dogs are his specialty. Possibly the most profusely spotted mammal in the world, the Catahoula (now called "Leopard Dog" by many) is the state dog of Louisiana, named after Catahoula Parish.

Sportsmen bring their Catahoulas from all over the state, hiring G.T. to train them to hunt feral hogs. G.T.'s even designed a special vest for the Catahoula that diminishes blows from big boar tusks to the dog's torso and neck. At four hundred to eight hundred pounds, a wild Texas hog can not only destroy crops, but they're also prone to destroy farm equipment. A critter with such a curious brain combined with that massive strength is bound to get into trouble.

Out east, a friend near Bells described finding a hog that looked closer to a thousand pounds, down in a deep draw on his property. During his morning coffee in the kitchen, our friend thought he heard a distant car horn honking in repeated, long successions. Fred raises a lot of heritage breed cows on a big place, so he's always wary of trespassers. He found the source of the honking, though the noise itself had stopped for at least half an hour. Sitting in the bottom of the draw was a 2001 faded red Ranger pickup. Two teenage boys were clinging desperately atop the roof of the cab. The Ford's fenders and tires were destroyed. The tailgate hung askew, and the doors were badly dented.

Pausing between sorties, the tusked beast glanced up to the crest of the rise, sighting Fred's truck. Fred said he was cleaning his rifle the night before, so had unfortunately left it at the house; though he would never have fired at the hog that close to the boys anyway. The nearly spent wild creature skedaddled for his own life. Fred rescued the boys and swore the rear axle of that little truck looked bent.

Vern is familiar with the thousand-pound hog story from his dad but doesn't know the boys on top of the truck who nearly met their maker. At the farm this spring, we hosted a cookout for Catahoula trainer Garland and some of his best customers. Annie and Clara were in charge of all the farm-to-table dishes, save the dark red, sweet and nutty wild boar chops that Vern helped me grill over mesquite charcoal lumps. The chops were marinated overnight in olive oil, with pineapple sage, crushed striped garlic, Hill Hardy rosemary, and lime basil, all fresh from the garden.

Vern is a bright kid, planning on being a vet someday. He's another teen recommended to me by the ag teacher at Elysia High. Though a reliable worker, his advanced placement course schedule allows only occasional hours at my farm. He calls me every weekend to let me know when he will likely be available for the coming week. Vern likes being around the assorted types of farm animals here. He talks to the animals more than to humans, actually.

Vern also has a crush on my daughter, Liz. If shy Vern happens to be working for me during one of her infrequent visits home from grad school, his painful silence is louder than ever.

In the driest part of this parched summer, Vern was truly a lifesaver. He was on the roof of the back porch, replacing some tiles damaged by recent high winds. I was below, delivering items up the ladder to him. I was hand-pumping air into a leaky, cracked tire on my rusty wheelbarrow when I thought I'd actually heard his voice from above. It sounded like he said simply, "Sam?"

I backed out from under the porch eave, and shaded my eyes from the noon-day sun to look up at him. "Vern. You say something?"

He pointed to the front horse pasture, east of the house, toward an odd sight. All the equine herd had nostrils raised high, all peering northwest, standing near each other. Even the old swayback fellow, saved recently from a life of isolation, stood as straight as he could, in rapt attention with the others.

A strong waft of smoke reached us. "C'mon down, Vern. We need to take a look." The lanky teen was down the ladder in an instant. We jumped into the old Rodeo and headed toward the front gate, which Vern opened and closed quickly. I got out. Looking in the direction of a couple of tandem smoke columns in the distance, I told Vern to climb up on the roof for a better look.

"It looks close to old Henry's place" the boy said.

We raced in the direction of Henry's few acres, about fifteen miles away. He had an old barn twice the size of his little rarely painted clapboard-sided house, a toolshed and a rickety carport that listed to one side. He had two-hundred-year-old blackjack oaks out back for shade.

Otherwise, his place was surrounded by miles and miles of prairie grasses and grains. In the country, people dream nightmares full of wildfires.

In route, I pressed the volunteer fire department number in my contacts list. Vern's dad answered. "G.T., I have Vern with me. We're going to see if Hank's OK."

"Good, Sam. The field just north of him was a small fire that we doused pretty quick. We've moved just half a mile south of his place. You'll see us. The wind's picking up a bit from the northwest, so hopefully it won't change course and bring the fire back across the bar ditch to him. But it's spreading fast down here."

"Was Hank OK?"

"He's worn out, but insisted we leave him for now. Last I saw, he was sitting down, still holding his garden hose at the ready. But I don't think he'll need it. Gotta go, Sam."

When we arrived, Henry's faded, two-tone station wagon was in the drive, so we parked on the road. In the distance, we could see G.T. and a couple of volunteers spraying the fire from two sides. They were using the big Type 3 fire engine, so would likely have plenty of water. Vern and I went around to the backyard to check on our old widower neighbor. Henry was slumped over, sitting on the ground, scared and shaking a bit. He'd been frantically spraying the back yard and tool shed with his garden hose before G.T. arrived. He was covered in sweat, ash, and water.

From the deluge applied by the fire truck, some water was still running off the field down toward Hank's exhausted figure. He clutched some old family photo albums to his chest, as he raised his weary head, acknowledging our presence.

"Sam, I don't think I can stand up." Henry said helplessly, hose still in one hand.

"That's OK Hank, we'll get you moved." Vern probably weighed no more than 140 pounds, so attempting to carry the spent but otherwise stout fellow all the way down to the road seemed unwise. Like many farmers, the top of his bald head was white as an egg, incidentally, from always wearing hats outside. I don't think I'd ever seen him without a hat.

Hank's normally sunburned face was pale, and I feared he was about to faint. Time was not on our side. I had the boy fetch Henry's metal wheelbarrow from the shed. We raised his soaked body off the dirt and lowered it butt-first, between the wooden handles, onto the wheelbarrow. Vern had smartly grabbed a couple of tattered seat cushions off the back porch to soften the ride. Still clutching the photo albums, the old man's short legs hung over the barrow's rim at the knee, as would a child's.

"Hank, we're gonna take it nice and easy. We're just goin' to wheel you out to the truck. You can lay down in the back seat. OK?"

"That sounds feasible," he said.

Speeding to Elysia, I handed my phone to Vern. He called the hospital to let them know we were on our way. A good kid, Vern reached back, keeping his hand on Hank's arm and side, bracing his old body all the way to town.

That night, I relayed all the day's adventures to Annie by phone.

She was back in Beaumont, continuing her research on the history and practice of rice farming in Texas. I was sitting up in bed, reading Emily Wilson's new translation of Homer's *The Odyssey*, when Annie called. She was reading it too, and we'd planned to discuss it, but the grass fire near Elysia was more relevant a topic that evening.

Old Henry was being kept overnight for observation, but his prognosis was good. G.T. and the volunteers had effectively stopped the grass fires. A heavy dew was kindly forecast for the next morning. Annie would "expect nothing less" than the bravery and competence demonstrated by young Vern that day. She thinks the world of that quiet, conscientious boy. On occasion, she advises me to not be surprised if a future match develops between Vern and my grad student daughter. Sometimes Annie teases me by referring to Liz as "...the older woman" in Vern's life.

Annie asked me to retell her the legendary story of Hank's little clapboard-sided house, saying she'd turn in for the night afterward. The house had belonged to Henry's older bachelor brother, deceased. When Henry's wife, Brenda, passed away, the loneliness in the big farmhouse they'd built together was too much to bear. He lumbered for days on end, up and down the long halls and felt lost in them. The house was too full of her, too full of their life together. His grown children had long since made their own far-flung nests and couldn't rearrange their lives to take possession of the big place, so Henry had sold the few acres around the house, and the house itself, to a young couple who were actually former students of mine.

Henry liked the compactness of his deceased brother's place, which was willed to him. It was perfect for his minimal needs. It was kind of like a row-house turned sideways, with the front door on the wide side of the house, right in the middle. It had a kind of sensible symmetry to it, Henry thought. And from the road, you couldn't really determine how deep the rest of the building was anyway. So it had the appearance of a broad, larger structure.

Henry's older brother, Nathan, was a tall, lanky farmer. He entered World War II at seventeen, a confirmed bachelor. He returned to civilian farm life that same bachelor, and never looked back. He was a quiet soul who just wanted to plow the land in a kind of meditative sense of gratitude for being alive. I had an uncle like that. Europe's battlefields were abominable corruptions of farmland, Nathan thought, manmade blights on God's gift. He just did his best, moment to moment, to be a good steward over what he could handle by himself. He figured he could be a better steward and have more immediate success, moment to moment, if he did it without a mate.

Nathan was a sound sleeper. He did not fret and roll on imagined stormy seas in bed. He was at peace with his life. Legend goes that he once slept right through the swift work of a big tornado that ripped his little clapboard house off its meagre moorings one dark night. Rotating the little building a few times, it was dropped gently out of the center of the vortex, like a cyclone's burp, landing in a neighbor's wheat field. Nathan didn't have a lot of belongings or possessions, but next morning he did notice that his breakfast table and chairs had moved snugly into one corner of his tiny kitchen.

My old friend, José Cantu, has been in charge of laying new water pipes at the farm, insuring reliable access for all the gardens, the two big chicken palaces, and all the livestock. José has built and converted and repaired garages, sheds, and parts of barns into functioning art studios for me, for many years. José can build anything. He has a mechanical engineering degree from Mexico and is a master at solving problems. Problems present themselves moment to moment at the farm, day and night.

José has a crew of painters he keeps busy restoring and main-taining various apartment sites in Tarrant County. This contract work allows him to continue working on individual projects with old clients like me. He says he likes challenges in his work, not monotony. I've certainly given him challenges over the years with issues over light-ing, storage, and gallery-type walls unique to art studios. When I'm unavailable, José sometimes brings his brother-in-law with him for two-man jobs. But José mostly enjoys working by himself. In this, he reminds me of many of my own farming relatives and artist friends. Farmers and artists have a continuous thought-line of concepts and issues, problems to solve, all the while physically producing something. Farmers and artists don't mind working and thinking alone.

At the end of the day, I'm always amazed at what José has accomplished. He works steadily, but never rushed or frustrated. He will sometimes come find me when he needs two more hands or another willing back, but these are short periods of interruption, with tasks executed in very few words.

One hot and still morning recently, José was upstairs in the studio building a new window seat and surrounding bookshelves. I shouted up to him, requesting his help downstairs in the tack room. The water heater was in the tack room, and José had routed lines for all the stall misters from that convenient source. The small pump and valve assembly that regulated the timing sequence and duration of the misters' spray was attached atop the heater.

"The misters have stopped working, José." I was sure he'd come up with a solution. I certainly was hoping to avoid having to order a new pump part and wait who knows how long for it to arrive during that endless heat wave. I went back to work in the adjacent feed room, while José examined lines and connections for a few minutes. In a short while, José stuck his head around the feed room door, saying "Señor Sam. Let me think about it."

He went back upstairs to continue working, cutting and installing the pieces needed for the handsome woodwork required for the window seat design. Later, we had lunch on the barn's covered side porch that looked out onto the front horse pasture. Over the weekend, Annie had made a batch of her remarkable chicken salad and baked a loaf of her delicious buttermilk bread. José and I enjoyed sandwiches of that, with some of our pickled watermelon rind from the pantry. We usually catch up on news with each other over lunch. José's wife, Mary, is a nurse at a hospital near Wichita Falls. His daughter is a biology major at Austin College in Sherman, on a girls fastpitch softball scholarship. He's proud of her, a southpaw, with a mean curveball. Annie and I have seen her pitch. She's as serious as her father when she's on the mound.

I finished my inventory in the feed room and was making notes on the wall calendar when I became aware of a presence at the door. I turned to see Sol's big head studying me. Sometimes he looks like a cartoon caricature with that huge head in proportion to his little body. That big head helps him squeeze through any gap left between the sliding wooden barn doors.

The look on Sol's long face portrayed his utter disappointment at spotting me in the feed room. I'm sure the miniature donkey's little brain was full of hope and anticipation, now completely dashed at the sight of my presence. "How tragic," he must have been thinking. After stealthily sneaking undetected into the wide hallway of the barn, his eyes widened at the open door to the feed room. I'm sure he had visions of unsecured lids on bins full of heavenly alfalfa cubes.

Sol is the eternal optimist. His little memory records many more victories than losses in his ongoing struggle to outwit me. With one eye on the bins, and one eye on me, he stood with front legs firmly planted on the raised feed room floor while his hind quarters were lower than the front, those hooves out in the hallway. In his mind I suppose this stance gave him the delusion that his whole body was all at once taller. He was watching carefully; I'm sure devising a counter-move to whatever action I was about to take.

I took a cube from the top of one bin, holding it up for him to see. No need to disguise the gesture, as Sol had reconnoitered the feed room's floorplan on numerous occasions. He knew the layout. I suspect he's able to loosen bin lids, using his prominent white incisors as pincers.

Sol backed into the hallway slowly, eyeing the cube in my hand the whole time. He followed me out of the barn and chewed pleasantly at the equine ambrosia I finally offered from my palm. I keep hoping I'll train him to sit for a treat. He's seen the dogs master that trick long ago. Sometimes the little ass is a slow learner.

The sun had fallen far into the western horizon, so I'd returned to the feed room to finish up, after closing the barn doors tight. José came to the feed room and asked "Señor Sam, do you have a ball-point pen?" I looked at the pen in my hand, asking, "Will this one do?"

"Yes," José replied. "You don't need it?" I picked up another pen for my use. José deconstructed the ball-point pen, removing the little spring inside. He held the spring up between his thumb and forefinger, calculating its length.

"Maybe," he said, while heading next door to the tack room.

I'd gone upstairs to check on the progress of the new woodwork. I liked the window seat assembly idea. The window in question faces north, so it has a great vantage point for the front gate and county road. The seat has a lid, with a storage compartment below. I heard José call me from downstairs. As I stepped down into the hall, I could hear the misters' spraying gently in the stalls.

José explained that a valve spring had worn out on the mister regulator, and the spring in the ballpoint pen was, with a little stretching, the same approximate size. We wished each other a good evening. I handed him a bag of cherry-husk tomatoes that I'd picked for Mary. She was on day shifts for a while, he said, so they were going dancing that night.

I'm not much of a dancer, myself. I have rhythm, but my feet have little to no memory. Annie is a very good dancer. I learned swing-dancing when in high school. My mother and aunts taught me to waltz and two-step as a kid, so I can blend in without too much damage on the dance floor. In other words, I don't embarrass Annie and me at wedding parties...much.

José's Chevy van pulled out onto the road and headed west into the sunset. Shadows were long at the farm. I opened the gate to the south pasture so that Sol could help Caesar bring the sheep in.

I could see Caesar's majestic canine stature in the distance. How could anyone miss him? He stood up tall, stretched his long white body into an arc, his big tail in the air like a flag. He looked like a curving ski-slope on the horizon. He yawned broadly. The sound of my unlatching the pasture gate had awakened him from his nap in the shade of a random willow tree.

I went back inside the barn to put evening meals into buckets and bowls for the horses and dogs. The stall ceiling fans were spinning. The misters were misting properly. All the stall windows were wide open. Barnes County residents and their animals breathed a communal sigh of relief as the big yellow paint-peeling sun slid over to the other side of the world.

~

My grad student daughter, Liz, came up to the farm from far East Texas about a month ago. Her graduate forestry projects and papers at Stephen F. Austin seem to take up much more of her summer days than undergrad school ever did. She stayed a week and enjoyed getting back into the rhythm of farm life for a little while. We hadn't seen Liz since early June, when we went down to Nacogdoches to celebrate the Blueberry Festival with her and school friends. Annie, my sidekick, though well into the last chapter of the manuscript on Gulf lowlands rice farming, took a few days away from the city to join us. She and Liz have always gotten on like a house on fire. They had fun preparing Annie's new rice recipes every night, and I always enjoy hearing their happy voices coming from the kitchen.

Upon arrival, Liz gave me a hurried hug and peck on the cheek, then rushed off to check on her precious loblolly pines. Obsessed with that beautiful East Texas tree, she is convinced that with the blend of loam and sand and the near perfect 7.0 pH of our farm's soil, her loblolly test will prove a success. I would be supportive, of course, even if she wanted to plant a stand of aspen.

Liz helped me raise the large pop-up tent I annually use for the hens so they have shade above their wading pool. Yep, a kid's wading pool. And the girls love it. Feathers get hot too, I suppose. While filling the big metal waterers for the heritage breed chickens, I asked Liz to remind me to check on our supply of electrolytes, which we add to the hens' fluid intake well into late September these days. For that matter, electrolytes for all your critters during the blistering summer isn't a bad idea. We still have plenty of scorching days left. Don't be lulled into delusions of autumn just because the last couple of days may have stayed below one hundred degrees.

José's superlative plumbing repairs on the outdated automatic waterers in the horse stalls are providing consistent, fresh H_2O to the equine boarders. It's like horse cocktail hour after their evening feed. Whatever amount the animal drinks is immediately replaced in the smooth basin with enough cool refreshment for the next long sip, and so on. With fans and misters in each stall, these horses have weathered the past several summers in style. As Uncle Buck Bartlett, the family's rodeo star, would have said, they've been living "in high cotton."

The heirloom tomatoes have been at their most flavorful here at the very end of the season. So many consecutive nights in the nineties did gardeners no favors, but the orange and red acidic beauties came through like gangbusters at last. My friend Sara, at her small, tidy farm near Muenster, produced some of the most unusual (hardest to grow in Texas) heirloom tomatoes I've seen, and they grew all summer. We concocted our own sea-tea recipe earlier in the spring, and she applied the mix to her tomato plants with the same frequency I used on mine. Our efforts have paid off.

Sara is not only an avid organic gardener, but she also has a large number of Araucanas, the handsome South American chickens that lay green and blue eggs. She sells to the public at her farm, from a pop-up tent by the road. Sara's shy and wouldn't dream of greeting customers at a big city venue. Whenever I'm selling at a farmers market near her place, Sara brings eggs and produce for me to sell at my stand. I know customers would love to meet her, but she's back in her old truck and headed home as soon as we've unloaded her delivery.

Sara called me during a recent reduction in egg-per-day output from her layers, so I agreed to come take a look. I love visiting her operation because much about her engineering and methods seem quirky to old time farmers, but her plants and critters thrive. For example, she grows watermelons on an old cyclone fence, supporting their weight in pantyhose tied to the metal mesh. I took a couple of watermelons from her vertical melon patch and fed the chickens with it. The hens perked up right away, naturally.

She was delighted with their improved appetites and when their normal laying pattern returned in a few days, Sara sent me a thank you note with some watermelon seeds tucked into the envelope. Of course, some of the prior loss of eggs could have been due to the seven-foot-long chicken snakes Sara admitted to pulling out of the coop two nights in a row. By the way, I don't "catch and release" snakes like Sara does. I'm frankly glad that my place is as far from hers as it is.

Some of the normally bullet-proof herbs have suffered from this year's hot summer. The delicate serrated-leafed salad burnet gave up way too early. The historic variegated-leaf blood sorrel, one of my favorites, has given up the ghost as well. The pineapple sage looks like it's been in a war zone. It has seemed parched at any time of the day I've checked on it for many weeks. I'm concerned that the plant may not even produce the beautiful long red petals (they taste as sweet as honeysuckle blossoms) that abound on their bright green leaves most years from late summer right up to early December. Annie has a recipe for pork roast that I love. Along with the usual garlic cloves, she fills slits in the roast with pineapple sage leaves.

As usual, the fat, round lemon cucumbers have been prolific and delicious this year.

Their gorgeous skin with yellow and white striations provides a pretty wrapping for the almost sweet, almost watermelon-like flavor of the pale-green interior, ending with a slight hint of lemon or citrus. The inner flesh of the lemon cucumber is the color of the lightest celadon ceramic. I feared that I had planted these favorite cucumbers too late, but they have thrived in the heat, growing up on strong Aromatto basil trunks and along a fence line at the edge of the garden.

I fertilized with organic sea-tea three times over about five weeks while the young plants spread their vines. I figured I'd done too much. But I guess with the barrage of heat waves assaulting them every day they needed the frequent boosts after all.

This year, for the first time ever, I planted poblano peppers in the garden. Poblano peppers become *ancho* peppers when dried and roasted. I love the flavor of poblano peppers when they achieve that dark, rich green color just before turning red. The morning or afternoon you see these splendid hot fruits turn red, take them, because they soften quickly. Poblanos, of course, provide the fuselage for the traditional chili rellenos.

If you like nachos or quesadillas or migas, try ancho peppers instead of jalapenos. The flavor of ancho is a natural companion to queso. I guess it's not unreasonable that peppers might like it hot, so they must love it this year in my garden. At least that what they seem to be telling me.

On a recent Sunday morning, I was concerned that I hadn't seen Nike for quite a while. Blackie was ever-present, helping me water the garden, water the chickens, even water her own hot dog body. I'm convinced she thinks her barking commands the garden hose to produce water. Elysia and environs have been set on "550/broil" for too long this summer. But Blackie's loyal partner-in-crime, my year-and-a-half-old Bluetick hound was nowhere to be seen.

I started looking in nooks and crannies of the green house and tool shed. Finally, back at the barn, I found Nike laid up in a hole in a corner of one of the stalls. She was in a recess carved out of the dirt floor by various critters (dogs, cats, a lamb or two) trying to get to cooler ground. I was shocked to find the pup's left foot swollen to the size of a baseball. It had split wide open, and she was bleeding from the gaps between her toes. She couldn't stand. She was so weak I was afraid she might die in my arms as I carried her to the Rodeo. I called Vet John at home. Thankfully, he answered, but got right to the point.

"For you to call me at home on a Sunday, I assume it's about another Bluetick." John and I, and Blueticks, have history. "Meet me at the clinic. Back door, as usual."

I laid Nike carefully in the rear of the Rodeo. Bracing her bony little body inside a canvas-tarp nest I made for her, we hightailed it to town. John was waiting for us, holding the back door open with his body. He gently rubbed one of her long ears as I carried her inside.

John said the makeup of all the serosanguineous fluid drained off Nike's foot was typical of snakebite. By the size of the localized swelling, his best guess was a copperhead. Good guess, as the recent demise of one of those dangerous little crawlers at the barn suggested it maybe had a partner or siblings. So Nike spent overnight Monday in town, spoiled rotten by John's staff, her every need attended to.

Nike can charm anybody. The intensity of her gaze is hypnotic, with those big Cleopatra-looking eyes, the long, velvety ears starting near the center of her head, like a pharaoh's cobra-shaped head-dress framing her handsome, long Roman nose. Nike's black spots on her coat look like the darkest, richest chunks of coal from a nineteenth century Welsh mine. All this, plus her affectionate nature, adds up to a very special animal. Even Elizabeth Taylor wouldn't want to be cast alongside this little mysterious, museum-quality Egyptian beauty.

As with many of our pets, I waited for Nike to reveal her own appropriate name. Clara, Vern, and other teen farmhands were growing impatient. Every now and then I'd catch a suggested name during their whispered debates, like Spot or Sally or Sacagawea. But the first couple of weeks I watched Nike bravely (and forcefully) defend herself as a child-pup against the ruffians Caesar and Blackie. These seasoned brutes love to wrestle like tough, ancient Greek athletes, throwing and pinning each other to the dirt. I decided she was pure warrior, a classical, unstoppable Nike the Victorious. She loved to stand her ground on the field of play-battle, even as a youngster.

The masterful incisions and healing treatment, plus the good-natured attitude of the willing invalid, proved therapeutic enough for me to return Nike to the barn. Blackie was elated to have her pal back. My plan was to keep Nike in the barn for a couple of more days, just to make sure the wounds had dried clean, and that the medications could complete their work. She wasn't interested in moving very fast in the midday heat of the barn anyway. Like us humans, I think Nike had begun to appreciate air-conditioning during her emergency vacation to the city. If Blackie was eager for Nike to wrestle, she didn't show it. She's had lots of litters, and being a good mother, she knows to be patient with children.

Speaking of patience, my good friend Bill Goodman has mastered the art. Shortly after returning Nike to the barn, I encountered one of those unexpected problems that occur with such regularity on the farm. I needed to replace one of the horse waterers, due to a raucous dust-up that developed when Blaze decided to interlope on Samson's stall. The younger gelding's oat-bucket raid provoked a hard-thrown left punch from big Samson's rear paw. The costly waterer couldn't move aside fast enough, so it bit the dust.

Each stall has a waterer, back-to-back, sharing a common wall, mirroring itself on the other side. So to replace pipe in one involves connecting the new pipe to two waterers, not just the one that's busted. José was supervising a big apartment project in Fort Worth for several weeks at that time, so was unavailable. Not being a plumber myself, nor much of a handyman for that matter, I naively figured to simply replace the bum waterer in one, easy in-and-out job with a new clone. Like replacing a float in a toilet. *Not.*

I'd already picked up the new waterer from Pete at the Elysia feed store. Now this was on a Saturday, mind. I picture Bill Goodman on a Saturday, sitting out under a big shade tree in his yard. Leaned back easy-like in his old metal lawn chair, feet propped up on the rear wheels of a riding mower he's repairing, Bill would likely be sipping a cold glass of iced tea. Having worked hard all morning, I could see him planning on a quiet, uneventful afternoon, contemplating a nap.

So I call friend Bill. "Bill," I say into the cellphone, "I'm in over my head on a plumbing job at the barn."

"Emergency?" Bill asks. I explain that isn't necessarily the case.

"No emergency. But José can't come out for a couple of weeks. It's a waterer I need to replace in Samson's stall. If you've got room in your schedule the next few days, I could really use your help. I've got the new waterer in hand." Samson is Bill's favorite horse. He's always appreciated the majestic way Samson carries himself without arrogance or attitude.

"Well, we can't leave the Gentle Giant in such a fix, Sam. Tell you what. I'll head that way now. Might take us into the night. But we'll get her done."

That's Bill. Like Blackie with her pal Nike, there's no hesitation on his part to leap into a big mess with a friend and tackle it together. No hesitation in his voice either. "I'll head that way now." Simple. Reassuring.

So on a blistering hot Saturday, I assisted Bill as he figured out exactly what we needed to do to install the new waterer and connect the new pipe to the corresponding waterer on the other side of the two-inch-thick wooden wall. We must have sawed and glued a dozen joints and elbows to get it done, but they all fit, were amazingly the right length, and soon the water flowed evenly, and all was right with the world.

Of course, Bill and I depended greatly on the assistance of good friends Blackie and Nike. The canine comic relief alone lightened our work. The two critters were constantly and literally underfoot, now sniffing and snorting at the cans of glue, then putting noses right in the paths of oncoming handsaws. Most of the time they just kept us company, laying in the cool pine shavings of Samson's stall. Their tails raised and lowered periodically, like the wave of a friend's hand, to let us know they were still on the job. Bill didn't get his nap that Saturday. The dogs did it for him.

Tunis lamb and ewe

Epilogue

ODYSSEUS WAS A FARMER

We sometimes forget that Odysseus was a farmer. He was probably a well-respected farmer in Ithaca, but I'm not sure of the county he and his young wife, Penelope, lived in. He was surely an admired man, a man with a respected history, lest Homer would not have made him a king.

Homer made him a king with a conscience who took responsibility for his actions and openly grieved his mistakes and failures.

Odysseus went to Troy with many other farmer/kings to rescue Queen Helen of Sparta from the clutches of Paris, the handsome Trojan prince. Paris had abducted Helen from her husband, King Menelaus, a wealthy sea-going adventurer. The Trojans lost the Trojan War. Odysseus rushed home, again by boat. The gods slowed him down.

Odysseus was a farmer, so it's understandable that he would have trouble at sea. The gods made sure of that, heaping trials and tribulations upon him during his ten years' long journey home. His return was made on deep water, not on *terra firma*. Like many of his fellow soldiers, Odysseus just wanted to get back to his farm alive.

Argos was the boon companion of Odysseus, before and after The

Trojan War. Probably a Laconian breed, Argos protected Penelope and their son, Telemachus, during the farmer king's absence. When Odysseus finally returns home to Ithaca, it is his faithful dog who first recognizes him with a heartfelt tail-wagging salute.

~

T hese days, the fat-tailed Tunis sheep are grazing on that portion of land I sat aside for native prairie grass restoration. The buffalo grass, little bluestem, big bluestem, Indian grass, and switchgrass have shown prolific growth the last couple of years. That acreage is like a nature sanctuary, enjoyed by countless butterflies, honeybees and nesting birds. The gently rolling terrain is now carpeted in tall and short green grasses. It is a bucolic sight. I can imagine the ancient ancestors of my Tunis flock grazing on grasses that Odysseus and Telemachus planted in Ithaca.

Anglo pioneers referred to the prairie grasses as "the grand ocean of the plains." They traversed the "seas of grass" in "prairie schooners." Let Walter Prescott Webb's *The Great Plains* be your guide for the flora and fauna and human actions on the American prairies. Many years ago, in meeting one of the new American history profs for the first time at a campus gathering, I happened to mention my admiration for Webb's work. The young man thought for a moment, then remarked, disdainfully, "Oh, yes. He was the *agrarian,* wasn't he?" Obviously, this fellow's students were going to be taught little or nothing about the importance of agriculture to history.

Technological progress does bring change, even here. The idyllic prairie farming community of Elysia is moving forward into the modern age. All the town talk of late has been about the installation of our first traffic light. Locals just call it "the red light." A supermarket being built out on the state highway apparently requires one.

Old Man Winter has been rearing his ugly head again, each day threatening something fierce.

Worries about portending weather have actually been tempered considerably, incidentally. I just got the news that my request for additional ag exemptions for heirloom herbs and produce acreage has been approved. Reluctant Bob came through after all.

It was becoming clear, on a recent afternoon, that Barnes County was in for a stormy ride, weather wise. The power had already stopped in Elysia and environs. I moved the big generator down to the barn to provide juice for some lights and one industrial-size heater in the hall. Annie, in the dark house, gathered extra blankets and pillows, wearing her bicycle headlamp. She looked like a miner. We keep a full-size camp air mattress upstairs in my studio, for just such events.

I'd just gathered the last eggs of the day, many from beneath hens who had already decided to bed down for the night. It gets dark so early this time of year. Even though I leave a light on in each chicken house for a couple of hours after sunset, I'm convinced the hens are on a natural rhythm that disregards my thoughtful provision of artificial illumination. It's pitch-black outside, so the hens ignore the light in the house, huddling together in twos and threes in the laying boxes for warmth. It's just too cold to roost, though they normally prefer to sleep that way. In summer, it will be just the reverse. Most of these lovely, heritage-breed chickens will be sleeping quietly perched upon the rails provided out on their airy, screened-in front porch, stacked in rows above each other. Turbines in the roof will spin, drawing out the warm air and filling the interior with cooler temps, as attic fans did in human houses when I was a boy.

But that evening, as night came on, the cold wind steadily picked up force. Chilling gusts were rattling the tin walls of the chicken houses. The turbines were still, their air passages sealed with plywood for winter. As usual, I made a last-minute inspection to ensure that the hot wires were working around the fenced yard. (Raccoons love chicken for supper, summer or winter). With all the feathered girls secured for the night, I double-checked that a small generator was running the heat lamps OK. I was ready to head down the hill to the horse barn and feed the livestock.

Before taking care of the poultry, I'd already ordered Nike, the Bluetick Coonhound, to "load up" into the old, rusted Rodeo (now the official farm-only truck). Even in winter, if I don't take control of

Nike at sundown, she will be out until the wee hours, howling at real, and imagined, wild critters up in the trees.

A cold blast nearly ripped the door out of my hand as I climbed into the cab, Nike sound asleep in a tight ball in the passenger seat. Snowflakes and sleet pellets swatted me soundly before I got the door closed. All of a sudden, snow and sleet blew down in great slurries, whipped into plumes and eddies of white by the strong winds. From the truck headlights I could see that much snow had already fallen while I was busy in the chicken houses getting everybody settled. The road and fields were already covered in a couple of inches of snow. As I rounded the key-hole shaped filtering pond, sliding a bit, I realized a thick layer of ice had formed before the snowfall.

As I made the circle around the pond, my neighbor's rank little Mexican bull stood forlornly by the fence, seeming to plead at me for shelter as he stared into my headlights. The neighbor's sad little herd never had shelter of any kind, and rarely much food.

Late at night I would sometimes sneak a bale of hay over the fence to two hungry cows. The neighbor was a proud, and private, weekend farmer. (His farm truck was actually a new hybrid SUV, which he drove out on Sundays to check on the place).

More snow than sleet was falling as I wound the slick, curving road back down the hill to the barn. Nike was unmoved. Far ahead of me, in the light of the barn-lamp above the sliding doors, I could see the equine gang, huddled together, jostling for position to be the first to enter the castle, the cozy horse-hotel called home. Sol stayed close to Samson, his huge body discharging more heat than Blaze. A dusting of snow powdered their backs.

Earlier that afternoon, alfalfa cubes in feed buckets and fresh hay had already been divvied up amongst the herd, appropriate for each animal's girth. Nike and I went in through the feed room door, avoiding the crowd of eager equine shoppers at the barn entrance. Out of nowhere, Caesar, the giant Pyrenees/Akbash combo, Spin, the blue heeler, and Blackie the mongrel piled into the barn hallway right behind me and Nike. Lots of appreciative tails were wagging in the warmth of the barn. I walked the length of the hall, checking to ensure that each stall door was wide open, ready to receive its hungry occupant.

On cue, the dog pack huddled on the safe side of the stairwell enclosure as I drew back the large sliding doors, welcoming the barn boarders. The ensuing stampede was but a couple of seconds. Each horse raced into its proper stall, apparently too wet, too cold, and too hungry to play games with each other that night. Steam rose from the moist snow melting off their big bodies.

Heads deep in buckets, their stall doors were closed behind them without incident. The cats at the other end of the barn had constant access to their feed pan inside the tack room, as the door stayed ajar just enough for their skinny bodies to slide through. They all slept pressed together in one mass near the water heater.

I fed the dogs in the hall, where they would bed down for the night. I reached through the narrow gap in the tack room doorway, lifting Nike's coat off its peg. The thin coon hound eagerly stepped into the coat, waiting patiently while I connected all the leg straps. Nike, compared to her furry running mates, looked little more than a balsa-wood frame with paper stretched over it, like an vintage model airplane fuselage. She had no layers of fat or thick hair on her skeletal frame. With no interest in wrestling or play-fighting that cold night, the dogs were soon curled into tight balls within their circular, padded beds.

In winter, I normally leave the stall lights on to protect the boarded horse's coats from becoming like wooly mammoths. I turned off the hallway lights, and the stall lights, to save energy. The dogs were already asleep. Outside, the wind and snow howled against the cedar-sided barn and rattled the sliding front doors. The sheep were huddled next to the barn, snug up under the deep paddock overhang, well secured against the night's windy assault.

Annie and I had anticipated a night in the studio. The roads were covered with inches of ice and snow, so we hoped that few people would be out that night. It could be especially dangerous on the state highway, since I doubted that the traffic signal would be blinking any to control traffic.

I followed Annie up the stairs into the warmth of the studio, which was provided by the old wood-burning stove near the bath and office. We both carried armloads of the storm disaster provisions. The large, flat iron plate on top of the stove was also our cooktop. Soon we had the kettle on, and water would be hot almost instantly. The whistle would let us know when.

The air mattress was near enough to the stove to benefit from the heat, even on nights when temps dipped into the teens. Annie was cozy in an old armchair, reading *The Odyssey*, illuminated by Granny's old floor lamp. It had a thin, very worn parchment lampshade with a faded print of grapevine leaves around it. Annie loved it.

I walked to the business end of the studio, performing a final parsing of the sketches I'd done for a new painting commission. The subject was a gingerbread-style cottage in silhouette against a star-filled night sky, with fireflies congregating around the front porch. It's odd how often I like to paint scenes out-of-season. I suppose it's a way of controlling the weather (in my head).

I went downstairs for one last headcount of critters in stalls, below. Sol raised his head at my approach, just to let me know he was still on guard. Blaze lay flat out, as was his habit, beside the donkey. Tall Samson was standing, sound asleep. The old, rescued swayback, who has yet to reveal his name, snored gently, warm in his new blanket. Dolly, the mare, rested peacefully beside her new foal that was not orange. Pickle and Tofu were down in Waco for some halter-class competitions with their teen owners, Clara and Margaret. The dogs weren't moving. I'd already set the alarm on my cellphone to wake me up at 2:00 a.m. to check on fuel levels of the generators outside. If any canine needed to go out to do their business, that would be the time.

But it was late. I was tired. Too tired to be hungry, I'd enjoy a cup of mint tea and hit the sack soon after. So I did little more than assure myself I was on the right track with the design of my new painting. No brilliant strokes to be added to the thing on that chilly night. I glanced over to see Annie's smiling face. With her eyes, she motioned toward the floor. There, curled up at her feet was the pretty hound, Nike. The lanky dog had stealthily climbed the stairs unobserved. She's no fool.

I chose the largest oak log I had on the woodpile upstairs and centered it on the hot coals. Closing the door, I turned down the damper. The log would simmer slowly all night, providing an effective, hot catalyst for a bigger, warmer fire in the morning. I slid under the comforter and blankets, falling fast asleep. The last sound remembered was that of Annie turning a page of her book, while fat snowflakes slapped at the studio windows around us.

Sol grazing

Recommended Reading

Hold Autumn in Your Hand, George Sessions Perry, (1941), 1950, Whittlesey House, McGraw Hill Co. Inc, New York

The Cotton-Pickers, B. Traven, (1926), 1995, Elephant Paperback, Ivan R. Dee Inc., Chicago

Corduroy, by Adrien Bell, (1930), 1986, Oxford University Press, USA

Farther Off from Heaven, William Humphrey, 1976, Alfred A. Knopf, Inc., New York

Train to Estelline, Jane Roberts Wood, (1987), 2000, Univ. of North Texas Press

Like Water for Chocolate, Laura Esquirel, (1989), 1992, Doubleday Dell Publ., New York

Tender at the Bone, Ruth Reichl, 1999, Broadway Books, Random House, Inc., New York

A Wood of One's Own, Ruth Pavey, 2019, Duckworth/Prelude Books Co., UK

Selected Poems, 1965-1975, Seamus Heaney, 1980, Faber & Faber Ltd, London, UK

On Farming (De Agri Cultura), Cato the Elder, (160 BC), 1998, Translation by Andrew Dalby,
Prospect Books Co., UK

The Great Plains, Walter Prescott Webb, (1931), 1981, Bison Book, University of Nebraska Press

The Mind of the South, W.J. Cash, (1941), 1962, Alfred A. Knopf, Inc., New York

The Points of My Compass, E.B. White, (1954), 1979, Perennial Ed, Harper & Row, New York

Wood Eternal: Osage Orange/Bois d'Arc, Fred Tarpley, 2010, Tarpley Books, Campbell, Texas

Seeds, Sex and Civilization, Peter Thompson & Stephen Harris, 2010, Thames & Hudson, UK

Catching Fire: How Cooking Made Us Human, Richard Wrangham, 2009, Basic Books, New York

An Edible History of Humanity, Tom Standage, 2009, Walker Publishing Co., Inc., New York

About the Author

T.D. Motley is a Texas painter and
academic. Born in Beaumont, he's
been drawing since age three. His
family has farmed in Texas from the
mid-nineteenth century. He and
artist wife, Rebecca, marketed their
organic, heirloom herbs and produce
to North Texas chefs for years.

Motley is Professor Emeritus of Art and Art History at Dallas
College. His drawings and paintings have shown in national exhibits
and are included in numerous U.S. and Texas collections. Motley has
lectured at the Dallas Museum of Art, the Umlauf Sculpture Garden
and Museum, Austin, Texas, the Meadows Museum at Southern
Methodist University in Dallas, and the Amon Carter Museum in
Fort Worth. He has published essays for museum catalogs, art period-
ical critiques and reviews, and National Endowment for Humanities
research papers on art and literature of the Greeks and Romans. He is
contributing author for Eutopia and ArtSpiel and has written about
mid-century modern Texas artists for DB/Zumbeispiel and the Grace
Museum, Abilene.

Motley has received Fulbright Grants to Belgium, the Nether-
lands, and the UK. He is past Board President of Artist Boat, a Galve-
ston non-profit, teaching students about coastal nature through art
and science. He was Chair of the North Texas Fulbright Teacher
Exchange Peer Review Committee for many years. Motley was a
printer in the U.S. Air Force, an illustrator for Ling Temco Vought

Corp, and a cartoonist for the infamous Dallas Notes from the Underground. Motley's artworks can be seen at J. Peeler Howell Fine Art, Fort Worth.

Looking for your next book?
We publish the stories you've been waiting to read!

Check out our other titles, including audio books, at
StoneyCreekPublishing.com.

For author book signings, speaking engagements, or other events,
please contact us at info@stoneycreekpublishing.com